"A wormhole is opening," Data said, "and there is a steep increase in radiation output."

Picard tensed. "Any signs that it's another ship?" he asked.

"Mass registering millions—no, billions of metric tons," Data said, and before anyone else could react, it rushed through the hole, quaking as it arrived. "Mass approximately equal to Earth's moon," the android added. "Diameter—why, it is smaller than the *Enterprise*, Captain."

Picard shook his head, slowly. "Not a ship, then. Tightly packed neutrons."

"Yes, a neutron star."

"Velocity, Data?"

"Approximately one-third warp speed, sir."

"Heading?" the captain asked, though he already knew the answer.

"Collision course with the Dyson Sphere."

DYSON SPHERE

CHARLES PELLEGRINO

AND

GEORGE ZEBROWSKI

POCKET BOOKS

New York   London   Toronto   Sydney   Tokyo   Singapore

This book is a work of fiction. Names, characters, places and incidents are products of the author's imagination or are used fictitiously. Any resemblance to actual events or locales or persons, living or dead, is entirely coincidental.

An *Original* Publication of POCKET BOOKS

POCKET BOOKS, a division of Simon & Schuster Inc.
1230 Avenue of the Americas, New York, NY 10020

STAR TREK is a Registered Trademark of Paramount Pictures.

A VIACOM COMPANY

This book is published by Pocket Books, a division of Simon & Schuster Inc., under exclusive license from Paramount Pictures.

ISBN: 0-671-54173-0

First Pocket Books printing April 1999

10 9 8 7 6 5 4 3 2 1

POCKET and colophon are registered trademarks of Simon & Schuster Inc.

Printed in the U.S.A.

*To Freeman Dyson,
who else?*

There are more things in heaven and earth, Horatio,
Than are dreamt of in your philosophy.
—William Shakespeare
Hamlet

God is in the details.
—Freeman Dyson

What we perceive about other creatures is often
delimited by our accustomed scale of size or time. An
adult mayfly, during its one day of earthly life, might
well view tadpoles as immutable species.
—Stephen Jay Gould

DYSON SPHERE

1

The Shape of Heaven

TONIGHT, CAPTAIN PICARD came back again to his mother's old admonition: "Be careful what you wish for, Jean-Luc. You may get it."

Sitting in his ready room, he again played the record of the *Enterprise*'s brief first passage through the Dyson Sphere. He had played it so many times now that his mind was numbed by it, numbed by what a later computer analysis of that scan had revealed. He had believed the Sphere's interior to be completely lifeless, but a detailed examination of the data by newer and more advanced computers had shown a variety—a nearly infinite variety, Picard supposed—of plants and vegetation.

But what they had at first concluded remained true: The Dyson Sphere had seemingly been abandoned by whatever life forms had constructed it. The later analysis had revealed no signs of higher life forms, of intelligent life.

Picard thought he knew every river, every stream, every wrinkle in the world's topography, but he understood that the Sphere's size was every bit as deceiving as it was overpowering, and that for all he thought he knew, there was infinitely more he did not know. The only objects the ship's recorders and the later computer analysis might possibly have missed were a couple of twenty-mile-long elephants. What appeared to be a braided stream was really a river wider than the Earth and descending more than two hundred million kilometers from its headwaters; gazing across whole light minutes of land and sea could draw even the most seasoned explorers into moments of madness.

Picard closed the record of the earlier passage through the Dyson Sphere and opened his captain's log to review the most recent entry.

CAPTAIN'S LOG, STARSHIP ENTERPRISE
Stardate: 47321.6

More than a year has passed since we found Montgomery Scott's ship, the Jenolen, crashed on the outer hull of the Dyson Sphere. More than a year, during which bureaucratic procedure delayed my plans for a return to the Sphere. We cannot go in until I have assembled my team of Federation-qualified archaeologists. I want scholars who are also efficient excavators—which means calling on the assistance of Hortas. They can move through rock as effortlessly as a man walks through air. Unfortunately, they are as stubborn as they are efficient—which has meant more bureaucratic delays.

Two science vessels met us at the end of our first encounter, met us near the Great Wall as we were departing; but the Federation had restricted their exploration of the Sphere entirely to surface mapping and long-range subspace scans. They were under orders not even to try entering Dyson.

Our previous method of entering and exiting the artifact had actually required the destruction of a vessel. The Jenolen held the door to Dyson open while we, in the Enterprise, just barely escaped, having no choice but to fire upon and destroy the vessel blocking our path. We found no obvious way of triggering the exit lock from the inside, and once triggered from outside, a vessel would be hauled in by automatic tractor beams, and the door would close.

Picard closed the log and rubbed at his forehead. He needed a break, a respite from Dyson's vastness, even if it was only a few minutes' escape to a cup of hot tea. Picard heard his mother's voice in his mind once more: *Be careful what you wish for, Jean-Luc. You may get it.*

He smiled to himself as he realized he was a latter-day Spyridon Marinatos. The legendary archaeologist would have appreciated Yvette Picard's warning, when during the summer of 1967 he tunneled into the lost city of Thera, making the discovery of his dreams, and realizing in that same instant that more than his entire lifetime would be required to excavate it. The city was buried under sixty meters of volcanic tephra, and it spread more than two kilometers wide.

Yet for all its overwhelming size, and for all of Spyridon Marinatos's dismay, Thera could easily have been flung into a corner and never found again, had it been situated near one of the "little" doorways that led into Dyson.

The Sphere was dead, of course. Every analyst had agreed on that much: Dyson was a ghost town built to psychopathic proportion, which gave the captain his long-wished-for kinship with Marinatos. He was, at last, being assigned his own archaeological expedition; but as he remembered how Marinatos had fretted over needing more than his own lifetime to discover and catalogue the artifacts of an extinct civilization, Picard wondered what his Greek predecessor would have thought of a ruin whose exploration might require more than ten *billion* lifetimes.

Be careful what you wish for—

Now, the *Enterprise* was approaching "the Great Wall of Dyson," about one hundred light years distant from the Sphere. It was a wall of stars—an actual wall, beyond which no stars at all could be found. No planets. No comets. No meteoroids. Nothing except . . .

Picard shivered, recalling his now prevailing, probably correct theory about what had happened to the hundreds, perhaps thousands of star systems that must once have existed on the other side of the wall.

Will there come a time when *we* know such power? Such arrogance? Picard wondered.

"We shall pass through the wall in fifteen minutes," Data announced over the deskscreen.

"I'll meet you on the bridge in five," the captain said and tensed for a moment, then shut the deskscreen off. He was suddenly and acutely aware that his fellow officer was, like the Dyson Sphere, but the handiwork of a clever species, of a momentarily very successful species, that might or might not become as extinct as the Dyson engineers one day.

Dyson was already an artifact. Data might yet become one.

Clever species, Picard thought, then thought again of all those missing stars between the wall and Dyson, and thought again of power and arrogance.

"What are we going to do with the universe?" he said to the empty room, and winced. "Wherefore, what shall we do?"

* * *

Charles Pellegrino and George Zebrowski

The universe was full of belittling timeframes. For the Horta named Dalen, the last third of her life, all of those years, had passed so quickly that they seemed only a Vulcan lifespan.

How many more years lay ahead? the Horta wondered.

Maybe fifty thousand?

Yes. Fifty thousand, perhaps, but no more.

This was a mere chip of time, scaled against the age of her homeworld, Janus VI, whose oldest rocks had solidified more than seven billion years ago.

"Only the rocks live forever," said the humans. She could scarcely dream what time must mean to them—to Picard, and to his predecessor, Captain James Kirk, whom her people would always remember as one of those who had brought them out of the darkness.

When Dalen's ancestors already had many millennia of history behind them, there had existed only a few thousand people on Earth, and they had scarcely begun to wrap their minds around the concepts of building huts and milking goats. Yet during the lifetimes of the oldest of the Horta, billions of them had come and gone. Whole empires had come and gone. And the humans, understanding, now, how to milk power from antiprotons and subspace, had come to the stars and showed no intention of ever going away.

And they had carried with them, in their first deep-range exploratory vessel, the Vulcan named

Spock, who was said now to be approaching the end of his own unimaginably short lifetime.

Captain Dalen, for her part, barely perceived the paradox. For her, there was only satisfaction in the realization that some part of the Vulcan who had saved her entire species—had managed to live a little while longer, if only in crude snippets of DNA.

A little while longer . . .

It was more than a thousand light years, the Horta knew, from her starship, the *Darwin,* to the Beta Niobe nova. Curiously, that distant sun could still be viewed starboard and aft, as a dim star circled by a thriving Class M planet.

To the Horta-turned-Federation archaeologist and starship commander, this was the best and worst of times. She oscillated wildly between regret at leaving her quiet life in the caverns of Janus VI, and celebration of escape from her quiet life in the caverns of Janus VI. She was getting used to discovering strange paradoxes in every direction, ever since the humans had opened up the universe to her people. A part of her hated them for this. And a part of her loved them for the same reason.

The surface of Captain Dalen's Homeworld had been nothing except the cold vacuum of empty space, and any who had tunneled straight up and broken through were gushed out, naked, onto an airless deathscape. For their efforts, they left behind only two things: a screaming, outgassing tunnel that had to be quickly sealed, and a very poor inducement for continued space exploration. The theologians and the philosophers around her had declared that there was nothing on the other side of the sky. All life, all matter, and time itself ended at a world-encircling ceiling. And beyond that: nothing. Absolutely nothing.

And then out of nothing, out of that deep, impersonal nothing, had come the miners and the explorers and the starships, bringing with them the tools of subspace communication—which revealed to the Horta a sky that was full of voices. There had been a time when a nest of newly hatched Hortas had seemed crowded to her, even intimidating. But nothing, it seemed, was so crowded as cold, "empty" space.

One of the most prominent of the latest generation of explorers was, unsurprisingly, also the newest captain of the *Enterprise*. This Picard fellow wanted to conduct an archaeological survey of the Dyson Sphere *now,* and he wanted the *Darwin*'s Horta crew on site *now.* And he had an uncanny way . . . of getting his way. Captain Dalen's shipping orders had come direct from Starfleet and the Federation Council in San Francisco.

She had no great desire to actually meet Picard. Clearly the man either didn't know or didn't care that Hortas always attended to the task immediately at hand before moving on to the next task, however long it might take. Hortas had the time.

Yet nonetheless she now found herself, her ship,

and her crew speeding through subspace toward Picard and the Dyson Sphere. And she had the feeling that whether it took her seconds or centuries to reach her destination two facts remained constant. One: Many of the Federation's assumptions about the nature and origin of intelligent life were, to her mind, probably wrong. Two: Many of the Federation's assumptions about the nature and origin of subspace were probably wrong.

It was nice to know that the universe still had secrets to tell, and that the humanoids, for all their great ships, for all their explored frontiers, were still eager to learn.

Compulsively curious species, the Horta thought, and winced. *What, ultimately, were the humanoids going to do with the universe? What would the universe do with them?*

"Captain," Data said, "the *Darwin*'s captain informs me that she and her ship will be coming through the Great Wall in three hours."

"It's about time," Picard said, and lowered a hand to his stomach. This time, his passage through the wall had produced a queasy feeling. At present, no dust particles glowed and scratched warp trails on the bridgescreen. Ahead of the prow, the nearest stars were two hundred light years away. This meant that in the view-forward, at normal magnification, there was absolutely nothing to be seen.

The captain had looked out across, and voyaged

across, thousands of light years without this same queasiness. He reminded himself that he had known the stars too long to be disturbed by dark, empty places; but little banana fingers were curling around his spine anyway.

This time, he knew that the emptiness had been engineered.

Last time, there had been nothing ahead except Montgomery Scott's distress beacon.

This time, he knew that the most impressive alien artifact ever discovered lay ahead; and while Dyson was huge by any standard, he knew that more than two hundred trillion kilometers of total darkness lay between the *Enterprise* and the Sphere, and that this, too, belonged to the artifact.

The Sphere was the only object of its kind in all the known regions of the galaxy, although Picard doubted that it was unique. It was simply too attractive a design possibility to have inspired the engineering prowess of only one intelligent species.

Data had named the object after the twentieth-century scientist Freeman Dyson, who had anticipated that some civilization, somewhere, understanding that most of the power from its sun was being poured, wastefully, into the unfillable sink of space, might contrive to enclose the sun.

When he first considered the idea, Picard had suspected that such a vast construction would have to be a Dyson Cloud—millions of closely spaced habitats clustered around the star, and therefore much easier to construct; but the reality had proved to be a continuous sphere of what seemed to be solid material, imprisoning its sun with no visible breaks in the outer surface—a delightful feat of engineering, using an advanced materials technology.

The artifact, itself two hundred and four million kilometers in diameter, was located at the center of a cave two hundred light years across. The cave was a perfect sphere carved out of the galactic cloud of stars, gas, and debris. There was no doubt in the captain's mind that the combined mass of thousands of solar systems had been gathered to open this hole in the galactic sea. Ahead, at the center of a stellar desert, was a vast oasis, watered by the energies of a once free star. Why then, as nearly as anyone had been able to ascertain, had the builders abandoned their creation?

With the wall of stars receding aft, the *Enterprise* began to cross the final hundred light years of desert toward the still invisible Sphere, and Picard could only wonder whether the presumed instability of the central sun was enough to explain why the builders had abandoned their home; he found it strange that they could not have stabilized the star before building so much around it. Was it possible that they had made the Sphere long before they suspected that their sun might develop problems? He found it difficult to accept that such a labor and resource-intensive project could have been undertaken by beings lacking in foresight, even though he knew very well that the psychology of intelligent beings was everywhere flawed. Curiouser and curiouser . . . it fueled his appetite for the mysterious; and between the desert and the central sun of Dyson, mystery was his only certainty.

He glanced at Deanna Troi, who was seated at her station to his left. She met his gaze in silence for a moment, then said, "I can understand your frustration, Captain. How can we believe that after so much work they simply gave up?"

"Or can we believe that they simply died before they could leave?" Picard answered. "Is it possible that they are still somehow here?"

He stood up and looked around the bridge. His chief medical officer, Beverly Crusher, had ventured up from sick bay only a few moments ago. She stood near Geordi La Forge, who had cleared the neutrino telescope display from his screen and was scrolling through a vast collection of high-resolution scans made during the *Enterprise*'s first, hurried visit into the Sphere. Viewed from a distance of more than forty million kilometers, there was a small white island on the inner surface, that later analysis by the more advanced Federation computer had clearly shown to be covered with Dalmatian-like patches of dark coloration. The patches probably represented forests and near-surface water tables interrupting what would otherwise have been smooth desert terrain. On Earth, Antarctica was considered large enough to be a continent. The desert "island" on Geordi's screen was six times as large, yet here it barely qualified as a beach.

Offshore lay a scatter of microscopic sandbars, ranging down in size from the British Isles to Manhattan Island. There were too many of these "true islands" to be easily counted, much less named. Some were heavily forested, and ground-piercing radar sensors had revealed narrow lines and rectangular depressions that might have been roads and building foundations, unrepaired for millennia. Other islands, at the very limit of resolution, displayed structures that still appeared to be standing intact, as if inhabited only centuries ago, or decades ago. And all of these lands were lost in the center of a strange sea, almost perfectly circular, and as wide as the orbit of Mercury. Geordi had named the sea Great Scott, in homage to his fellow officer and Starfleet engineer Montgomery Scott, the man whose crash beacon had first led the *Enterprise* to the Sphere.

Geordi turned toward Picard. "I'm with you, Captain," the chief engineer said, "I can't believe that they just left all of this behind. They built a sea wider than four thousand Earths. What happened to them? I can't help thinking it must have been a terrible accident of some kind."

"Hard radiation could have left the Sphere intact," Data said, "while destroying all life. Maybe their sun flared suddenly, driving the creators out and producing a barren landscape resembling Earth after the death of the dinosaurs."

"But some of the islands appear to be covered with highly evolved forests," La Forge objected. "To judge from the heights given by radar imagery, we're talking about trees—big trees—possibly even with animals in them."

"The forests could have come through a disaster by the dormancy of their seeds," Data pointed out. "Or they might even have evolved afterward from mere grasses, or from lichens, and a few other stragglers that managed to hold on. The situation here may be similar to what a dinosaur would see, if it could be brought back to Earth today."

Geordi let out a laugh. "You mean, 'Look what happens: I go away for a few million years and the rats take over—and they've *evolved!*'"

"Exactly," Data said. "So I would not throw the catastrophe theory overboard quite yet."

"Perhaps the Dyson inhabitants were not driven out by anything," Troi suggested. "Maybe they found something more important to do." More important, Picard thought, would have to be *vastly* more important to qualify as a reason to leave.

"Or something less appalling to do," said Beverly Crusher. "I find this place extremely fascinating but still disturbing. To build something on such a scale—eating up whole sun systems in the process. What could have moved them to do it?"

"That," Picard replied, "is one of the things I hope to learn." Disturbing did not seem an apt characterization of the artifact; neither did bizarre. The words just weren't big enough. The right words, he decided, simply did not exist.

"Captain," Geordi said from his station, "I don't think there's been enough time for trees to evolve from grasses. That would have required millions of years, but if you look at the cave of stars—"

Geordi brought the view-aft onto the right side of the bridgescreen. "You'll notice that—" the engineer began.

"—it still has a clearly defined edge in all directions," Data finished for him.

Data marveled at the sharp edge revealed by the viewscreen. It was moments like as this that made the android long to be fully human. While the humans envied his positronic memory that contained the accumulated knowledge of multiple civilizations, he was not as skilled as they were at connecting disparate and seemingly unrelated facts. And he sensed something that might be called envy for them, envy for their gift of intuition, as he waxed encyclopedic: "Aft and ventral, Alpha Powell A and Beta Noyes C are moving toward the Great Wall at 5.3 kilometers per second. The normal motion of stars in the galaxy should have blurred the wall's edge relatively quickly, in the same way that constellations will change in the sky of any world in a matter of a few tens of thousands of years."

"I see," Picard cut in, "that such blurring is not even visible here—"

"Yes, Captain," Data continued. "This cave hewn out of the starfield cannot be much more than a hundred thousand years old, so by association the Sphere is the same age. As stars measure time, the Dyson Sphere was built only yesterday."

"Built by whom?" Picard asked. "That's what troubles me. Is there a race we know that could trace its ancestry to a people who would scoop out a volume of space two hundred light years across to complete an engineering project?"

"Captain . . ." Troi began, her voice laced with hesitation and concern.

"Yes, Counselor. Think of people with a voracious appetite for power. We must consider the possibility that this is the archaeology of the Borg."

"A fascinating hypothesis, Captain," Data said from his station.

"And like most hot speculations, it's probably wrong," Picard replied. "But criminal behavior does spring to mind, despite the impressive display. An inside-out world with more habitable area than a quarter billion Earths—it makes me think of all the solar systems that will not be here to develop intelligent life."

Troi said, "Perhaps it was guilt over that very realization that led to the Sphere's abandonment. That guilt may have worked on them for a long time."

"I wouldn't count on that," Picard said. "I wish I could believe that they became, like the Ionian Greeks, a race of philosophers and dreamers, and turned their back on instrumentalities." He shook his head. "Maybe the ultimate consumers went at last to another extreme, and threw off all material possessions. Maybe, instead of the Borg, the road to Dyson leads to—"

"No, not the archaeology of the Q," Troi said.

"A cosmic joke, either way."

"Captain," Data said, "we have few facts from which to reason."

"Quite right, Data. But the possibilities are finite. We can guess the answer—but it will only be helpful if we can later prove it true."

"Humans find it helpful to work in that way," Data said, "backward from a guess. Your great physicist, Richard Feynman, advocated such a procedure."

"But you find it . . . confusing?"

"A leap into the dark, perhaps," Data replied.

By the time the Sphere became visible as a pale gray dot on the main screen, Commander William Riker had come onto the bridge. He, Data, and

Geordi La Forge had reviewed all the known facts about the artifact, and had begun to connect them with incoming information.

Picard leaned forward in his captain's chair, considering what the three officers had said, fascinated by how the real world had invaded the realm of possibility and exceeded all expectations.

The trail of neutrino flux measurements, recorded during the *Enterprise*'s first departure from the Sphere, out to a distance of one thousand light years, had confirmed that the star at the Sphere's center was in every way a normal, stable sun of approximately 0.5 solar masses. That had been true until only a few weeks prior to the *Enterprise*'s first encounter. Now solar activity was suddenly waning, bringing on a "Little Ice Age."

"Mr. Data—what's your diagnosis?" Picard asked.

"Curious, Captain." Data turned in his seat to face Picard. "There are indications that energy is being transferred through subspace to the very inner surface of the Sphere, causing the entire shell to move."

"What?" Picard asked. "Why would it wish to move?"

'I doubt that it wishes anything, Captain. It just does. Not only is the Sphere moving off center of its cave of stars—incoming neutrino scans now reveal that its central sun is also off center."

"Yes," La Forge said from his station, "I see it, too."

Picard stood up. "Is the Sphere malfunctioning?"

"Perhaps," Data replied. "Untended automatic systems will probably descend into chaos, given enough time. And it would seem to me that the Dyson Sphere has had enough time. There may be nothing at all intentional about what is happening."

Crusher left La Forge's side and came to stand near the captain, her eyes on the forward viewscreen. Picard suddenly felt that the vast construct, for all its frightful majesty, for all its obscenity and beauty, might be doomed; and it disturbed him to think that all they might have learned from it would be lost. If there was anything more disturbing than having the Sphere snatched away before his questions could be answered, it was having the Sphere snatched away before he knew even what questions to ask.

"Captain," Data said, "we are registering unusual activity deep inside the cave, at bearing forty-five mark five. On screen now."

Picard stared into the dark, but all he could see was a faint, computer-enhanced rippling of otherwise flat spacetime geometry.

"What is it, Data?"

"One moment, Captain. I must make certain."

"Very well, Data, but don't take too long."

"A wormhole is opening," Data said, "and there is a steep increase in radiation output."

Picard tensed. "Any signs that it's another ship?" he asked.

"Mass registering millions—no, billions of metric tons," Data said, and before anyone else could react, it rushed through the hole, quaking as it arrived. "Mass approximately equal to Earth's moon," the android added. "Diameter—why, it is smaller than the *Enterprise,* Captain."

Picard shook his head, slowly. "Not a ship, then. Tightly packed neutrons."

"Yes, a neutron star."

"Velocity, Data?"

"Approximately one-third warp speed."

"Heading?" the captain asked, though he already knew the answer.

"Collision course with the Dyson Sphere."

Picard sat down, stunned by the sheer weight of the numbers. An amount of mass small enough to be contained in a teacup, if converted instantaneously into photons of light, could vaporize a whole city. Even a crate of teacups, striking Dyson at relativistic speed, would have jarred the structure; but a whole lunar mass? This was far beyond overkill. In the arena of relativistic bombardment, a direct hit was as good as a glancing blow. At one-third warp speed, nearly a quarter of the neutron star's mass would be converted into energy, and a nearly equal amount of Dyson's mass would be converted. For several tenths of a second, Dyson would produce more light, and more fast neutrons, than all the stars in the galaxy combined.

Picard did not want to be anywhere around, on, or especially in Dyson when that happened.

And it really was going to happen, he realized.

He was powerless to prevent it. As he looked around the bridge, he could see the apprehension and frustration on the faces of his fellow officers. Worf, in particular, wore a grimmer scowl than usual.

"But why?" Riker asked from his station.

"Perhaps someone doesn't approve of Dyson Spheres," Picard said.

Troi asked, "Is it possible that the race that built it is now destroying its work?"

"Perhaps they have enemies—" Worf said, clearly seeing the neutron star as a weapon being wielded, "—who will not tolerate such a display of power and craft encroaching upon their progress."

"Or," Picard began, "they have indeed sent a neutron star to destroy their own work after abandoning it, because they do not wish to leave such an artifact to be inherited by others."

"Build your own," Riker added. "Is that what they're trying to tell us?"

"If I may venture a . . . *guess,*" Data said, in what seemed an effort to show that his internalization of human ways was improving, "using even a whole Federation's worth of warp drives, it would be nearly impossible to push a neutron star up to one-third warp speed. But our sensors have detected, from a very safe distance, a black hole weighing in at fifty million solar masses swallowing whole star systems near the galactic core. As they fall, they spiral in, and these spirals are very tight, and very fast."

"Relativistic," Picard said.

"I have clocked neutron stars near the hole at one-third warp. All you need to do is open up a wormhole, and point it in the right direction."

"It acts as a cannon," Worf said, unable to hide the note of admiration in his voice.

"But that requires going to the galactic core, doesn't it?" Riker asked.

"I should think that would be child's play for Dyson's engineers," Picard replied.

"A cute trick," Troi said. She leaned back in her seat and shook her head. "But isn't it possible that the Sphere was abandoned to avoid the very danger we're now witnessing? What if it became too big a cultural target, too large an advertisement of power and ability, and some other race has decided to destroy this threat to its own existence?"

"I could not have said it better myself, Counselor Troi," Worf muttered from behind her.

"Pretty bleak," Beverly Crusher said. She turned toward Picard. "I suppose this can't just be a natural occurrence?"

"It is not likely, Dr. Crusher," Data answered. "Of that we can be certain. The neutron star is too well aimed, and its means of arrival too novel, perhaps even too well-timed."

"But what could they have feared from the builders of the Sphere?" Crusher asked. "Or from us?"

"Perhaps nothing more than that they would be destroyed if they didn't destroy first," Picard said.

"An old story," Troi added.

CAPTAIN'S LOG, STARSHIP ENTERPRISE
IMPACT MINUS 13 *DAYS*
EGRESS MINUS 10 *DAYS*

Who are they?
What do they want?
Why are they doing this?
I regret that we will probably never know.

Who would have believed, a year ago, that after tens of thousands of years of existence, the Dyson Sphere had only a year to live? What can be said, now, but that the universe has a severe sense of humor?

This time, the Enterprise will not venture inside the Sphere. A Voyager-class vessel, the Darwin, will join us for the purpose of exploring seas and continents and ruins, and to find a routine for entry and exit; but neither ship shall venture close enough to be seized by the lock's tractor beams until the system is understood.

For all our efforts, these last sixteen months, we have had only one glimpse of the interior.

But—oh, the things we have seen in that glimpse. Beautiful things.

Originally, our forthcoming reconnaissance of the interior was to have lasted six months.

Then the sun turned out to be moving off center and we were down to perhaps a month of exploration before staying inside ceased to be an option.

And now—now it's down to days. 13.6 days before the relativistic cannonball strikes. Already, that is too close for comfort. Long before that time, we must be out the door, and then we will lose Dyson, and I am afraid we will never see the like of it again.

2

Horta in Command

"CAPTAIN," DATA SAID, "the *Darwin* and her commanding officer, Captain Dalen, are hailing us."

"Open," Picard said.

The image of a Horta seated in the command pit of its specially adapted starship was at once disconcerting and delightful to Picard: a rock in a saddle. The Horta community had come a long way since first contact with the Federation, partly through the efforts of the legendary Spock. Despite their physical peculiarities, some of the Horta had become explorers.

Inside those lumpy, physically rigid shapes lived imaginative, supple minds that also wondered and were curious about the universe, that gloried in the means supplied to them by the Federation, and looked outward from the stony tunnels of their world.

"Captain Dalen here," the Horta's electronic voice sang. "Captain Picard, we must enter the Sphere as soon as possible, if we are to learn anything at all before it is destroyed."

"With all speed," Picard answered, trying not to smile at the irony of his colleague's new urgency. Rumor had it, Dalen had previously been irritated by Picard's eagerness. "Data, what's your latest estimate on the maximum amount of time we have?"

"Still holding at just under two weeks, Captain," Data said from his station, "including a three day margin for retreat to a safe distance from the blast."

Just days, Picard thought, to study the inner surface of a world whose Great Scott Sea alone was too large to run a sailing ship across in less than a century, where populations of tens of billions could conceivably live and never meet. Here was a vast archaeological universe, one that would haunt explorers for a thousand years to come. How much could really be learned during the single fortnight remaining?

"Captain," the Horta sang, "do you have any ideas about how to solve the lock triggering problem?"

"Mr. Data," Picard said, "may we have your thoughts?"

Data continued to face the forward screen, and

said, "Yes, Captain. The simplest solution to the problem, short of finding and replicating whatever combination of electromagnetic and or subspace emanations from our ship activated the lock last time, would be to send either a probe, or one of our shuttlecraft, to trigger the lock, then let it withdraw after the *Darwin* has entered. We are already running such a frequency search program, but it may be that a robot probe's mass will not be noticed by the system, and a shuttle will have to be used. It may also be that there is no combination of frequencies for triggering the lock, and that the Sphere's systems simply recognize and bring in vessels of a certain size and configuration, as it did with us on our last visit."

Data paused, then said, "Something is certainly wrong with the Sphere's exit program. When you see a sun going off center, it is a sure sign that the system has become unstable. So we must plan as though the doors of Dyson will slam shut after the *Darwin* goes in. When the *Darwin* wishes to come out, we will again approach with a probe or shuttle and turn the lock."

"I wish it were easier," Picard said.

"The time allowed us here," Captain Dalen said from the screen, "precludes a more elegant way. Going in poses no great difficulty for us, but coming out dictates in no uncertain terms that your *Enterprise* keeps station outside the Sphere. The only alternative is to probe the lock itself for a subspace pattern, or a code, if one exists, that we would use from inside to let ourselves and the *Darwin* out."

Picard shook his head. "That may take longer than the time we have, Captain Dalen."

Data turned to face Picard. "I must remind you, Captain, that we cannot use weaponry to open the lock. The Sphere is sheathed in a membrane of solid neutronium."

"But the neutron star will penetrate it?"

"Nothing can stop such an object," Data said.

"Captain Dalen," Picard said, "some members of my crew will be aboard your vessel shortly to assist you."

"We're prepared to receive them, Captain Picard. Don't take too long. *Darwin* out." The viewscreen returned to normal.

Picard looked around, then stood up from his station. "Time now to decide which of us will go aboard the *Darwin*. Conference in five minutes."

Lieutenant Worf took a seat at the conference table, then looked around at his fellow officers, wondering if they truly felt the danger that now faced them. The frozen smile on Dr. Crusher's face was a sure sign that she was trying to push that danger to one side of her mind. Worf preferred to confront it.

Worf turned toward the head of the table. "Permission to speak, sir," the Klingon said to Captain Picard.

The captain nodded in his direction. "Go on."

"I do not believe," Worf continued, "that the Sphere is being targeted by a weapon. Stimulating as it is to consider such a war technology, I doubt that the Dyson Sphere merits an attack on this scale." The natural universe, as every Klingon knew, was itself a fearful antagonist.

"So how do you explain it?" Picard asked.

"Perhaps a natural catastrophe at the center of our galaxy opened this wormhole and brought the neutron star here by chance."

"Mr. Data?" Picard asked.

"That is possible, Captain, but not probable. Dyson has been here for as many as a hundred thousand years. The chances of the spontaneous appearence of neutrons now, during our visit, is at least as improbable as drawing a straight flush."

Riker shook his head. "In hindsight, every hand is equally as improbable as a straight flush—or, for that matter, a royal flush. Each one of those hundred thousand years was equally improbable."

"True," Data responded, "but while it may be a mistake to ascribe intent to an event that happens to concern our interests, in this case the possibility of it being an unintended event seems unlikely to me. In either case, we cannot proceed on that assumption."

"An accident of nature." Riker sat back in his chair. "It's just too convenient," he muttered.

"It seems convenient," Worf emphasized, "but only the most cowardly antagonist would hurl so massively destructive a weapon, even after a declaration of war. There is little glory in such conquests, and no chance for a warrior to display his bravery." He preferred to believe that what they were facing was a natural event, not out of any cowardice—he could hardly imagine such a contemptible feeling—but because standing against an enemy with such overwhelming technical superiority would require no ingenuity, no brilliant use of strategy and tactics, only the willingness to die for no end.

Picard rested his hands on the table top. "I understand your feelings, Mr. Worf," the captain said, "but this does bear the mark of an intended act. We cannot conclude, and behave, as if this were a natural occurrence in the absence of further evidence. While it may be difficult, at this point, to tell an intended attack from an accident of nature, we lessen our risk if we are prepared for the former and the latter turns out to be true."

"It is safer than the other way around," Data said, nodding his agreement.

The captain nodded back and said, "Now, Data, how many solar systems do you suppose existed here before the Sphere was built?"

"I estimate between one hundred and forty-six thousand and one hundred and fifty-two thousand, Captain."

"As I see it, that makes about one hundred and fifty thousand possible reasons why someone might have a grudge against the Dysons. Maybe one of the old evictees, or survivors, has come back. For all we know, what we're witnessing is one small battle in a galactic war. I'd hate to learn that the front line is coming our way."

Riker's eyes went wide with disbelief. He shook his head in denial. Worf was already wondering what kind of battle they might face.

"Be prepared for surprises, Number One," Picard said. "They're the only certainty here. In less than two weeks, all hell is going to break loose. And when it does, hell itself will look like shore leave by comparison."

Troi's fingers tightened around her cup of tea. "Or like Dyson but a little colder," she added.

"The front line?" Worf said, wishing that a Kling-on vessel were nearby, if only to gather what information it could about any advanced weaponry.

Picard looked grim. "That's one of the things we must determine, if we can, and if there's time— which brings up the question of who will make up the away team that is to go in with the *Darwin.*"

Crusher and Troi looked at the captain expectantly. La Forge and Data were still, while Wil Riker, with his familiar look of anticipation and restlessness on his bearded face, was clearly hoping to command the away team. They all wanted to go; they would all be thinking of what they might discover inside the Sphere. Worf was still contemplating the neutron star that might destroy it.

Picard turned his head toward Riker. "Number

One, normally I would put you in charge of the away team, but in this case I shall assume that position, and leave you in command of the *Enterprise*."

"I expected that," Commander Riker replied, but he looked disappointed nonetheless.

Worf knew what was coming next. "And since the neutron star is out here," Picard continued, "and since the Sphere's interior seems less likely to produce work for a warrior, Worf will remain outside with you. Data, you will also stay, and take charge of perfecting our method of entrance and exit from the Sphere."

"So who else is going?" Beverly Crusher asked. "You might need another physician aboard the *Darwin.*"

"If you had experience treating Hortas as well as humans, I'd agree," Picard said, "but I'd rather have you aboard the *Enterprise* for now."

Data said, "Then by process of elimination, Captain, it must be La Forge and Troi who will accompany you."

"Yes."

Worf heard the excitement in the captain's voice, and noticed that Troi was looking at him as if to ask how he felt.

"I'm fine," Picard said, as if anticipating her question. "Just had a physical last week." He glanced at Crusher, who nodded. "I must admit that I am excited by the prospect of exploring the Sphere. Thrilled, if I may say so. I wish our circumstances were less apocalyptic, but this is the hand we've been dealt, and there is no reason not to play it out. Does anyone disagree?"

Once again, Worf knew why he liked to serve with Picard. The man was not a coward; cautious only to the point where less caution would make him foolhardy; brave even to death if that were the right course.

"Well, then," Picard said as he stood up. "It's time to kick the door open. Data?"

"Yes, Captain. I shall make it so."

Worf's eyes narrowed in admiration. Once Picard had glimpsed the interior of Dyson, even with a relativistic shotgun aimed at his head, it was inconceivable that he should not go inside again and take a closer look.

"There is gold scattered under our beds," wrote T. E. Lawrence of his archaeological villa in Babylon. Picard knew this particular tale of Earthly archaeology well, and was reminded of it as he materialized aboard the *Darwin*. Thomas Lawrence and Leonard Woolley had provisioned their villa with a huge fireplace, ankle-deep sheepskin rugs, coffee tables with ancient Babylonian sphinxes for legs, and a huge bathtub with beaten copper trim. They ate dates from a golden dish found in the tomb of Shubad Khan, and drank tea from Hittite clay goblets. When a visitor asked them if they were worried about dropping and breaking the treasures, Lawrence (who happened, at the time, to be wearing a Babylonian king's robe of gold and silver thread) replied, "If we drop them, the British Museum will be glad to have the pieces."

That was about five years before World War I. Picard could get extremely depressed thinking about the archaeological treasures that had vanished during Earth's world wars. Much about the science of archaeology had changed since Lawrence's time, except for occasional intrusions of warfare into one's research—and, of course, the villas. They were, compared to the tents that botanists and paleontologists traditionally camped in, luxurious.

Picard nodded at the Horta positioned behind the lowset transporter console as he followed another Horta out of the transporter room, trailed by Troi and La Forge. The science starship *Darwin,* in a tradition dating back to Lawrence and Woolley, had been spared no expense. She was a giant, roving archaeological villa with warp engines and a pair of new, oversized shuttles attached to her belly. The shuttles, christened the *Balboa* and the *Engford,* gave the outside of the Voyager-class vessel, to Picard's mind, a curiously pregnant appearance.

Inside, as he had been informed, all of the decks, save for the engineering sector and a few dozen cubic meters of hastily furnished "humanoid quarters," were a maze of tunnels and bare chambers hewn out of what appeared to be solid rock. Picard, lengthening his stride to keep up with his Horta guide, felt

DYSON SPHERE

almost as though he were moving through a mine shaft. But it only appeared so.

"To the bridge," the Horta said when they came to the lift. Picard entered with his two officers; the door slid shut behind them. In a few moments, the door in front of them whisked open.

The *Darwin*'s bridge, even with its rocklike floor, stations with saddles instead of chairs, and consoles and display screens closer to the floor than usual, was not unlike the bridge of the *Enterprise*. The distant, only dimly lit Dyson Sphere had grown to cover the entire forward view of the wallscreen. Dead center, a subspace beacon dropped by the *Sagan*'s captain called attention to the only truly useful point of reference on Dyson's otherwise craterless, colorless surface. When Montgomery Scott's ship, the *Jenolen*, crashlanded on the Sphere, it had produced a thirty kilometer-long stain, or skid mark. This was the only sign of anything like a meteorite impact in all of Dyson's history. Even at the screen's highest possible magnification, there was no evidence that the crash had done the slightest damage to Dyson's shell. What appeared to be twin furrows of plowed-up debris had come, all of it, from the sandpapering the *Jenolen*'s underside had received; but the skid mark provided an unmistakable reference for orientation, making "Scott Base" the declared South Pole of Dyson. True as a compass needle, the skid pointed the way to the lock that Picard had opened once before.

Charles Pellegrino and George Zebrowski

Captain Dalen tilted the view upward from Scott Base. Upward and upward, revealing a landscape that, though he had seen it before, still seemed impossible to Picard.

The *Darwin* was a half million kilometers above Scott Base, approximately the height of the Moon over Earth. Dyson's horizon was many millions of kilometers away; yet the surface, which Picard knew was curved, seemed as level as the Utah salt flats viewed from the height of a footstool.

Picard walked toward the Horta captain's command pit, with Troi and La Forge just behind him, descending a rocky ramp to the captain's side. He straightened his tunic and said, more stiffly than he hoped, "Captain Dalen, on behalf of myself and my team, we are honored to be aboard your ship."

"Thank you," the Horta's amplified voice replied. "Together, we shall prevail in our mission. Please sit down, if you wish."

"Oh, I don't mind standing," Picard said. Except for the floor, the only other unoccupied and available seating at the moment was an empty saddle to the right of Captain Dalen.

"Enterprise to *Darwin.* Data here."

"Yes, Data," Picard replied.

"We are almost within sight of the lock entrance," Data's voice continued. "I think we can open it by tuning its subspace frequencies. I have now run through just over ninety trillion new subspace sequences. Statistically, we should be able to hit the right one by the time we face the lock."

"Continue," Picard said, knowing that what "should be" and what "would be" could be galaxies apart. "We can't let the system lead us in until we know you'll be able to open it later."

The lock was now visible on the screen, unchanged from the day Picard had last seen it. The *Darwin* and *Enterprise* both came to a stop and kept station with the lock's position. Both ships were well removed from the triggering point, where tractor beams would reach out and bring them inside.

Picard waited for Data to call. A minute went by, then another.

At last Data said, "It is taking longer than expected, Captain. Unlike our 'real' universe, subspace is not limited to just one electromagnetic spectrum. We have known of a hundred twenty-seven possible microverses. Here, I am beginning to suspect more."

The Horta captain shifted uneasily in her saddle. "How many more?" she asked.

"I'm seeing traces of thousands," Data said. "Multiple thousands."

Picard wondered if, after all their patience and planning, they would be unable to get inside. The neutronium membrane could, in theory, be pierced, perhaps even peeled back; but the damage would be horrendous. Although this would be nothing compared to the damage the neutron star was about to inflict, there were certain aspects of the Sphere's present instability that, at least on a subconscious and purely instinctive level, gave him the feeling Dyson was in some manner responding to the attack.

On the heels of this thought came an even more disturbing one: Might the previous instability have occurred in *anticipation* of the star's arrival? This meant that the presumably abandoned system was acting out of a sense of self-preservation, as he or Data would under similar circumstances. Increasingly, Picard was getting the impression that what he was really attempting was to enter a living organism—which meant that the *Darwin* and the *Enterprise* were, by comparison to the Sphere, a pair of invading virus particles. Viruses could survive well enough inside a human body, so long as they did not step out of line, vandalize any cells, and trigger an immune response. But—

No, Picard thought. Using the *Darwin*'s weaponry on the membrane would not work. The subtle approach, namely lock picking, would have to serve; although he had to admit that a meeting with Dyson's antibodies, if such existed, would certainly be interesting. He did not expect, however, that he would survive the encounter for more than a few milliseconds.

No, he reminded himself; we must be subtle.

"*Darwin* must be subtle," the Horta said suddenly, as if reading Picard's thoughts. "Then again, I wonder if our tunneling enzymes could eat through neutronium."

Picard was startled by the suggestion, but then realized that the Horta was not serious.

Captain Dalen was joking.

Picard let out a laugh, for polite show.

"The Sphere, the Sphere," Captain Dalen intoned. "Here is a question. How many Horta would it have taken to hollow it out?"

"How many?" Picard asked, knowing that he was being set up.

"One big Horta!" shouted Captain Dalen.

Picard laughed a little more loudly. Not half bad, he thought. Much better than "Horta Culture" jokes involving rock gardens.

"Captain Picard," Data's voice cut in, "I believe we have a subspace lock combination. It is spread across three hundred different subspace spectra."

"So it *is* an expanded microverse," Picard replied.

"Yes. It appears everything we thought we knew about subspace and superstrings will have to be rethought. The microstructure of spacetime is more tangled here than any place else in the known universe."

"The Sarpeidon Nebula," the Horta said, deadpan. "There is one other place. The Sarpeidon Nebula. We had an extended research mission there a little while ago."

"The now destroyed home system of a vanished

race that built time portals," Data shot back, obviously having made the connection in an instant. "And you say subspace is just as tangled there?"

Captain Dalen moved the entire forward portion of her body, approximating, in accordance with human custom, what Picard recognized as a nod.

"Are you suggesting," Picard said, "that the Dysons disappeared into time the way the Sarpeidans did?"

Captain Dalen shook her "head." "Unknown. We found that the tangle—well, sort of unravels about one hundred thousand years ago, as if it suddenly came into existence out of nowhere. I've been making modifications on the *Darwin*'s subspace sensors ever since, and so I've now had an opportunity to probe backward through subspace all the way from Sarpeidon to here. And do you know what I've found?"

"Let me guess," Picard said. "The Dyson tangle unravels near 100,000 B.C., which is about the time the Sphere was built."

"Correct."

"So, the Dysons, and someone on Sarpeidon, may have re-engineered the fabric of spacetime. Rebuilt it to their own design."

"Not just here and at Sarpeidon," the Horta replied. "All of the normal subspace dimensions between here and Sarpeidon have something in common with Sarpeidon and Dyson."

"You're joking," Picard said.

"Not this time. It's only a theory, of course, but Sarpeidon and Dyson—although the subspace that surrounds them appears to have been more intensely reworked than elsewhere—may not be merely the exceptions that prove the rule. They appear to be the actual rule. Probe back just a little way beyond them and all of subspace—all of subspace—breaks down into only the four most basic dimensions of space-time. I believe that someone, somewhere, rewove the entire fabric of the universe, and what's happened here is that you, and all the other young civilizations—maybe even the Dysons and the Sarpeidans—simply stumbled upon the bales of fabric someone else left behind, and learned how to wrap warp engines, transporters, and subspace communicators around them."

Picard looked at the Horta with astonishment and admiration, and more with admiration than astonishment. He let out a long sigh and said, "So, what you're suggesting is that subspace may itself be an archaeological artifact."

"May be," the Horta sang, and laughed.

"So then the question is, why would they build subspace so much deeper here?"

"There are many possible reasons," Data suggested. "One obvious advantage is that it greatly multiplies the odds against someone just cruising up to the front door and being able to find the right lock sequence."

"An added layer of immune defense," Picard

added, "probably against unwanted visitors, and unwanted infection."

"Meaning us," said Captain Dalen.

Picard grinned, in the manner that Sejanus, the Roman conspirator, might have grinned when he realized that the Emperor Tiberius had clothes after all, and brains, and teeth. "Data," he said, "try the lock twice. I'd like to know we have a good chance of making it work on our way out."

"I was thinking of trying it three times, Captain."

"Three, then."

"Signal sent."

The door to Dyson began to open, and Picard recalled that it was not the usual kind of airlock, since there was no atmosphere that could escape during the entrance or exit of vehicles. Dyson's atmosphere clung to the vast inner landscape, held in place by a field of pseudo gravity whose grip weakened so rapidly with increasing height that at an altitude of only fifty kilometers, it exerted no measurable influence at all. The doorway had a field of its own: a force wall standing thirty kilometers high and completely rimming its eight corners. Against that wall, the atmosphere piled up, as if it were merely water pressing against the sides of a fish tank.

The artificial gravity was not generated by centrifugal spin. It was created by gravitic generators, according to scans obtained during the first encounter. Much like the synthetic gravitational fields inside the *Darwin* and the *Enterprise,* they acted with little regard for the inertial effects of acceleration and deceleration—another fact made possible only by the miracle of subspace. This held true, of course, only for objects, or gases, or people standing within the field, which explained, without a doubt, the world's increasingly off-center sun.

"Lock closing, now," Data called from the *Enterprise*'s comlink.

Picard was looking straight ahead into brilliant sunlight, looking across tens of millions of kilometers of empty, airless space between Dyson's shell and a sun that, had turned inexplicably treasonous. The door's levers began to eclipse it, like the lids of a giant eye slowly shutting. And then the light went out, went out utterly, because the nearest star shining down upon Dyson's outer shell was one hundred light years away.

The darkness did not last very long. The *Darwin*'s photomultipliers were capable of looking down from the surface of Earth's moon and discerning the glow of a firefly in the Australian outback. They came on instantly, and the flattest plain in all the known universe was visible again. As Data double-checked and quadruple-checked his figures, calling out the results of his calculations from moment to moment, Picard looked forward to being on the underside of that plain. The *Darwin*'s time here would be too short, but he wondered if some bit of knowledge might be gained to prevent the coming destruction. It seemed unlikely, but he could hope.

"Lock opening again," Data announced.

After a second closing, and then a third, the Horta captain said, "Open again, Data. We'll take the *Darwin* in and try opening the lock from inside with the combination."

"You have it now, Captain Dalen," Data said.

As the lock opened, the Horta ordered half-ahead on impulse power. The *Darwin* eased forward, and entered the Sphere. As the ship continued forward and came around to exit, large land masses and bodies of water swept across the screen, spread across the incurving surface in full daylight. The lock was closing again as the *Darwin* came to face it.

Picard tensed, remembering the catastrophic exit of last time, when the *Enterprise* had fired upon the *Jenolen* as it held the lock open, beamed Montgomery Scott and Geordi La Forge out only a moment ahead of the ship's destruction, and then slipped through the closing lock at the last instant. That had been too close a call.

"Opening signal sent," Captain Dalen announced.

Picard took a deep breath in the seconds before the lock responded, then breathed more easily. As the *Darwin* came out, Riker said from the *Enterprise,* "Now I'm sure you'll stay to the last minute, or you wouldn't have made so certain of your exit."

"If it works four times," Picard replied, "it should work when we need it."

"Not necessarily true, Captain," Data said, "but very likely. Inductive reasoning is always a gamble, logically speaking, however small."

Riker said, "Inductive reasoning is often throwing your hat over the cliff and jumping after it."

"One more try, then," Picard said, "but this time we're going in for the duration."

Riker was becoming uneasy, increasingly so, as the others aboard the *Enterprise* wished the *Darwin* "good luck" or "Godspeed" and a "safe return." He did not like such farewells; they sounded like a challenge to fate. They made him think of others who had said the same timeworn phrases to people they would never see again.

At last, thinking of the Great Scott Sea, and all the other bodies of water inside Dyson, Riker recalled another kind of good luck message.

He leaned over his console. "Don't get your feet wet," he said to Picard and the others aboard the *Darwin.*

3

Transit of Darwin

THE SPHERE'S LOCK closed again. Geordi, sitting aft of Captain Dalen on the bridge, monitored from an engineer's station as the *Darwin* went forward. His console and display screen were nearly identical to his bridge station aboard the *Enterprise,* except for being closer to the floor so as to be more easily accessible to a Horta. He was sitting on one of the Horta saddles, which had turned out to be more comfortable than he had expected; at his right, Lieutenant Kar, one of the engineering officers, sat in front of another console.

Slowly the lock opened, and the ship entered the great lighted space.

"Darwin to *Enterprise,"* Captain Dalen said over

the subspace link. "We are safely inside and proceeding sunward."

"Reading you clearly," Data's voice replied.

"Captain Picard," Geordi said, "we've just picked up an anomalous gamma ray flare, but it's not from the sun. One Gev, precisely—meaning proton-antiproton annihilation. I'm seeing an apparent antimatter engine burn near an Earthlike planet orbiting some seventy million kilometers from the sun—planetary period, some two hundred and twenty-five days. And there's something else, Captain. A moon, thirty-three hundred kilometers across, coming around the far side of the planet."

"Full impulse ahead," Captain Dalen said.

Geordi looked up from his equipment, realizing suddenly that he had been addressing Captain Picard and not the *Darwin*'s captain; but he saw from the expression on Picard's face—a slight flush in infrared—that he should let the error go this time. He nodded back, then turned again to the instruments.

As the distance to the planet diminished, and the gamma ray source swelled on the *Darwin*'s viewscreen, Geordi noticed from the readings on his console that there was something familiar about the continents and oceans on this star's only natural satellite, and suddenly he understood what he was looking at.

"Captain Picard," he said excitedly, and then,

"Captain Dalen, the surface features of the planet ahead are the same as those on the inside of the Sphere! The builders apparently projected large the features of their own world." He put the forward screen into a quick three hundred and sixty degree sweep to illustrate the fact.

On the world below, and in the sky above, the Great Scott Sea was unmistakable—circular and huge, as one might imagine the eye of God. Geordi supposed that it must originally have been an asteroid crater, bigger than Earth's so-called dinosaur killer, bigger than the Great Hudson Bay. Flooded for more than a billion years, it had held sway as the homeworld's most dominant geologic feature, until its offspring projected it onto a surface larger than some planetary orbits.

"Further evidence?" Picard asked.

"Further evidence that the Dysons did indeed enclose their original sun when they built the Sphere," Geordi replied.

"And they kept their homeworld," Captain Dalen added.

"Perhaps out of aesthetic, or even sentimental reasons," Troi said; she was seated on a cushion at the Horta captain's right.

"Yes, very likely," Picard said from his seat near the Horta helmsman, "since to keep the world meant setting aside materials that would have contributed to the building of the Sphere. It was a deliberate choice not to use up their original world. Do you hear that, Data?"

"I agree, Captain," Data answered on the subspace link.

"I assume that you would wish to take up an orbit around the planet?" Captain Dalen asked.

A surprising reading suddenly came up on Geordi's scans. "Captain . . . Dalen," he said, "that world's moon: It's mass is much too small for a solid body. It has to be hollow. *Has* to be."

"Lay course for the satellite," Captain Dalen ordered.

"Aye, Captain," the Horta helmsman answered.

Far astern of the *Darwin,* Data tested the lock again, flooding the bridge of the *Enterprise* with the sapphire-orange glow of a low mass flare star. He adjusted the lighting, now that he knew precisely where to look. The off-center sun and the double world that orbited it were blue-shifting slowly but ominously toward him. *Wheels within wheels,* Data thought, recalling the words of the ancient Earth prophet Daniel. And here he was, looking upon a hollow sphere, orbiting a sphere, within a hollow sphere.

By his command, the giant levers began to close again; and before the doors shut out the light completely, his screens pinpointed and enhanced the signature of the *Darwin*'s impulse engines.

When he knew where to look, and how to look, the engine burn was just barely visible, scratching a thin veil of antimatter flame and subspace distortion across the face of the sun. He watched proton-antiproton exhaust eclipse fusion; he watched the starship *Darwin* in transit of Dyson's star, and in his head he recorded it—all of it—and at that moment he had an odd sensation, a sudden conviction that he might be seeing the *Darwin* for the last time, that like the *Flying Dutchman* and the *Mary Celeste,* the *Challenger* and the *Intrepid,* no ship would ever again bear the name *Darwin.*

A strange group of associations, Data thought. This was what human beings meant when they talked of feelings of foreboding, or of being "spooked."

Data wondered why. Perhaps it was the very vastness of the Sphere, into which a tiny speck like the *Darwin*—or the *Enterprise*—could so easily disappear and end up traveling for eons, like a ghost ship, without ever finding its way out again. Certainly, the loss of any ship was one of many possibilities, nothing more, but it seemed, at that moment, that he was watching the last of her.

As the *Darwin* settled into orbit around the alien moon, Picard saw on the forward viewscreen that its surface was a smooth eggshell finish. There were "dust" particles clinging to the shell—bundles of heavy helium clumped together with carbon isotopes and other residua of the solar wind. No signs of cratering, however. No meteoritic debris of any sort. Of course not. Every chip of ice, every interplanetary pebble, had been swept up in a cyclopean construction project.

"No sign of an entrance," Geordi said from his bridge station aft.

"What did they do, seal it up?" Picard asked.

"It seems that way."

"Or the entrance is expertly hidden," Picard suggested.

"We may not have time to find it," Captain Dalen said.

Picard nodded agreement, and said, "Then we should take one of your shuttles down to the surface and see if we can break in."

"Ah," Captain Dalen said. "After a few weeks of ceramic foam and false granite, my crew will be more than ready for a new flavor."

"It may be a surface that even a Horta can't eat through," Picard cautioned.

"We will see if that is true. Horta can synthesize what may be needed, and walk through."

It still startled him, from time to time, to think that Hortas thought of "walking through" solid objects. It was their physical heritage, of course, but something in the way Captain Dalen had spoken made him think that she was also trying to make another obscure Horta joke.

* * *

51

"I know you're sorry not to be going with us," Picard was saying to Troi, "but I should leave one member of my crew here, and you are the obvious choice."

"Of course," Troi said. She knew why; more time spent with other members of Captain Dalen's crew would give her more familiarity with their emotions, with what was normal for them. Neither protocol nor standard procedure required her to accompany Picard and La Forge to the shuttle entrance, but she had been picking up some disquieting sensations from Captain Dalen. That was yet another reason for comparing with other members of her crew what she sensed inside the Horta commander.

The shuttle hatch was already open, and Troi noticed that the interior of the shuttlecraft *Balboa* had seats suitable for humanoids as well as saddles for Hortas. Captain Dalen's pilots were already aboard the shuttlecraft. For her away team, the captain had brought along Lieutenant Jee, introduced earlier to the *Enterprise* officers as a "young archaeologist." Two other Horta officers, Lieutenant Sherd and Ensign Kodo, completed the team. Picard and La Forge greeted the Hortas, then followed them into the shuttlecraft.

Troi stepped back as the *Balboa*'s hatch door slid shut. She had picked up that same disturbing sensation again, and from all of the Hortas present this time. Anticipation, curiosity—those expected feelings were there, but she could also sense them in

Captain Picard, in Geordi, inside herself. Something else tinged the feelings she was picking up from Dalen and the other Hortas, a kind of reckless ecstacy, almost a mania, a lust to embrace the unknown.

The feeling faded. Troi told herself not to jump to conclusions about a species she had encountered for the first time so recently. But what she had felt suggested that the Hortas might be too quick to rush into dangerous situations in order to satisfy their powerful curiosity, and that, she knew, could endanger this mission—and all of their lives.

Moments later, the shuttlecraft *Balboa* was skimming low over the alien moon.

"Still no sign of an entrance," Geordi observed. Indeed, his surface scans had failed to reveal a seam small enough even for a virus to squeeze through. "It really does look as if they deliberately sealed it off."

"Were they trying to hide something?" Picard mused.

Data called out over the link: "It is always perilous to ascribe motives to an alien species, Captain."

"Quite right, Data. So we've little choice but to go in, assuming we're all curious enough."

"Oh, I think we're curious enough," Captain Dalen said.

"I certainly am," Geordi added, wanting to explore as much of this engineering marvel's interior as possible.

"Set us down, then, Mr. La Forge," Picard ordered, then glanced with obvious amusement at the Horta archaeologist saddled beside him, like a royal rock on display in a museum.

Their first landfall in the Dyson Sphere seemed straightforward enough. The *Balboa*'s docking tube would form an air-filled path to the moon's surface, and Captain Dalen's four-Horta away team would simply "walk through" the crust underneath, thus causing the least possible amount of damage to the structure, and Geordi hoped, setting off no alarms. On the other side of the shell, there was atmosphere, cold but breathable. Geordi had dropped two walnut-sized probes on the surface. The Hortas would survive inside, he knew. The sensor readings told him so.

He swept the *Balboa* into a graceful arc, as if it were a helicopter, then slowed to a hover, flashed his molecular strobes, and landed so gently on the moon's equator as to leave its thin veneer of helium-three "dust" undisturbed.

"Start drilling," Picard said. Geordi began to hope that Horta saliva would be enough; this sphere was not sheathed in carbon neutronium, which gave him a clue as to why it was here, and why it was sealed up.

"We're attached," Geordi said. "Horta entrance now open, and something like bedrock is below us, at least thirty meters of it, then topsoil. That's what my readings say."

Lieutenant Jee said, "I will walk through first." Her amplified voice was slightly higher than that of Captain Dalen.

Jee and the Horta captain, followed by Sherd and Kodo, slid ahead of Picard and Geordi into the shuttle's service bay, where a double-sized manhole led down to the moon's surface. Jee and Dalen sank away the moment they touched the ground. The other two team members fell in quickly behind, examining the shaft as they descended, shoring up the walls wherever it seemed necessary. Alice's fall down the rabbit hole had been much easier, Geordi thought, but the Horta captain seemed to think nothing of it.

After a few minutes, Geordi saw a circle of red light wink on at the bottom of the well. It winked out just as suddenly, and he realized that Lieutenant Jee was coming back up.

As she neared the exit, the Horta cried out, "Confirmed—human suitable atmosphere inside! But dark. Red dark."

"So how was it?" Picard asked, and the Horta's answering shudder reminded Geordi of a shrug.

"It was delicious!"

4

Contagion

THE HORTA HAD made their first landfall thirty minutes before. Now they stood, hard as it was for Captain Dalen fully to accept the reality, on the inside of a sphere—*topsy-turvy*—inside another sphere—*topsy-turvy*. The world within the world reflected only the longer, redder wavelengths of light. The weak red light was overpowered by black shadows; and, although she could not see them, vibrations in the ground permitted her and her team to feel strange shapes trying to move secretly forward and back in the dark. So far, they seemed to be keeping their distance; but until Picard arrived with reinforcements, Dalen had decided that she and her Hortas should cluster together, hold their ground and, as the humans would put it, be steady as a rock.

There were no life forms here other than plants. So the scans had shown. Dalen did not want to remind herself that, before they had been run through that new Federation computer, the first scans of the inside of the Dyson Sphere had revealed no life signs at all.

"Curiouser and curiouser," as the captain of the *Enterprise* was so fond of saying. Does he really understand how much curiouser this gets? Dalen thought, and should I tell him?

To begin with, there was the problem of similarity versus identicality. In spite of the Sarpeidan and Dyson quantum spacetime anomalies, as near as Dalen's crew could tell, every electron and proton in Dyson's hull was identical to every electron and proton everywhere else in Dyson, and everywhere else in the universe. In physics, the sameness of the individual bends in spacetime that built quarks and gluons and beget protons was absolute sameness, a sameness very unlike Data and his "identical" twin brother, unlike any two of the insulin molecules that ran through Picard's veins. Though similar, it was impossible to make any two androids or insulins absolutely identical.

And why is this? Dalen thought. "Why," she said aloud, "are all protons, for all their infinite opportunities for uniqueness, exactly the same? Why all electrons? And neutrons?"

The other Horta seemed unsurprised by her sudden questions, but then they were all undoubtedly brooding upon the same matters as she was.

A long time before, as Picard and his species measured time, the human physicists John Wheeler and Richard Feynman had theorized that every proton was identical to every other proton because there was really only one proton in the entire universe. In this case, it simply raced back and forth in time, again, and again, and again—appearing to show up everywhere at once. Starting off from the Big Bang, it would be shooting through Dalen's present, where she might catch a glimpse of it in Data's fingernails, or in Picard's insulin, or in Dyson's rivers, before it bounced back from the remote future and reappeared in her present as a proton moving backward in time, where some distant corner of the universe, or the antimatter pods of the *Darwin* and the *Enterprise,* would perceive it as a forward moving antiproton, before it reversed course, again, from the Big Bang. This being true, the same would hold for all the anti-electrons coursing through Data's positronic brain.

Wheeler and Feynman had buried their theory, or so those human physicists had thought. And then the discovery of subspace had made spacetime itself a cosmic free-fire zone. And now the discovery of subspace anomalies, Dalen mused, had made all things possible.

Was it possible, now, she asked herself, that a

proton bouncing back from the future could dictate
the present?

Yes.

Was it possible, then, that the present could dictate the past?

Oh, yes.

"I can picture it, now," Dalen said, suddenly
wanting to share her insight with her sisters and
comrades, "one antiproton and one positron in all
the universe, running head-on into the proton and
the electron at the bridge of time, at the moment we
call the Big Bang, thereby guaranteeing that the
universe will be created."

Sherd, Jee, and Kodo were silent for several moments. Then Sherd said, "Is it possible, then, that
whoever created subspace planned it that way—
perhaps even tampered with the manner in which
the Big Bang would occur, reshaped the cauldron of
creation?"

"Yes," Dalen answered. "I believe there has been
a great deal of tampering; more than any of us may
ever realize.

CAPTAIN'S LOG, STARSHIP ENTERPRISE
IMPACT MINUS 12.5 *DAYS*
EGRESS MINUS 9.5 *DAYS*

*Dalen Base was established only twenty minutes
ago. My chief engineer has confirmed for Cap-*

Charles Pellegrino and George Zebrowski

tain Dalen that the moon has its own subspace anomaly—which acts as a defensive barrier against our transporters. The Dysons made sure to button this place up tightly. Luckily for us, they did not anticipate Hortas. Captain Dalen's away team has saved us hours, perhaps a full day of work. Still, we may have to move even faster than I had hoped.

Data tells me that the larger Sphere is accelerating, and if one watches very carefully, one can actually see the Great Scott Sea moving perceptibly nearer. On the Sphere's walls, we cannot discern any inertial effects whatsoever arising from the acceleration.

On the wall opposite Great Scott, however, on the side moving away from us, the sacrifice to inertia is already horribly apparent. The landmasses there are turning white under the retreating daylight. Probably for the first time in Dyson's history, water is crystallizing out of the atmosphere. If the retreat continues, the air itself may eventually flow liquid, then turn to sand.

How strange that the first snowfall should come to Dyson, now that it is so close to the neutron flame.

Not much time left.

The hole in the moon had been cut at a forty-five degree angle, so it was possible to slide part of the way, in the direction that a sixth gravity would present as "down." But after a point, the gravitic direction reversed to "up," and Picard knew that he would emerge onto the inner surface of the sphere at four-fifths Earth gravity. Both he and Geordi were wearing traction soles and gloves, in case it became necessary to brake or climb.

"Ready?" Picard asked.

"Lead the way, Captain," La Forge replied.

Picard went in head first, and saw at once that the slide was slow enough to make braking unnecessary. He slid along slowly, feeling his way down toward the dim red light, and the opening grew larger. After twenty seconds he stopped, feeling the increased gravity in his heavier limbs.

"Mr. La Forge?" he asked.

"I'm right behind you, Captain."

Picard started to pull himself forward with his hands, then pushed with his feet. He was now climbing. He pulled himself along for what he estimated were about three minutes until he was at the opening. Grasping the edge with both hands, and pushing with his feet, he climbed out of the hole, sat down on the edge, and rolled away to one side.

He stood up and surveyed a dull red landscape. It was rocky and barren, save for a small stand of trees and bushes nearby, and similarly colored patches on the upcurved horizon. The trees were bare—dead, apparently. Geordi climbed out and stood next to him, and they looked up at a miniature red sun, radiating its pitiable energy into the hollow.

The Horta away team was waiting for them. "Air seems dusty," Picard said, and exhaled a cough that, in the surrounding atmosphere, became a breath of warm condensation. "Low oxygen, too."

"This *was* deliberately sealed up," La Forge said. "The Dysons must have seen this place as a failure."

"That sun," Picard said. "I'll bet it's artificial, and they couldn't get it to work, so they continued by enclosing their natural sun."

"No," said Captain Dalen. "I think this was all a test. A practice sphere, if you will."

"Could be," Geordi acknowledged. "It strikes me that they were looking far ahead. When this moon was constructed, all those missing stars and planets were probably still visible in the homeworld's night skies."

As Picard's eyes adjusted, he started to see by the red light. The curve of the inner land swept away from them in all directions, revealing a craggy, pitted, desert interrupted by distant oases of oddly shaped trees. More than a thousand kilometers away, lay the nearer shore of a circular sea whose center was located almost on the far side of the sun. It was the same continental and oceanic contour he had seen on the two worlds outside. It was the Great Scott Sea writ small.

Peering upward and seaward, Picard became aware of a sharp clicking noise, then noticed that some five hundred meters away, the rocks seemed to rise and move forward.

"Do you see that?" La Forge whispered in the redness that seemed to belong to some hell at the end of time. Then he began to scan with his tricorder.

62

"Yes," Picard replied.

"Definitely biological, with no implant modifications." The engineer turned in a circle, penetrating the gloom with his visor. "They shouldn't be there, but they are."

"Biological life forms," Dalen said. "I was afraid of that. The Federation had better think about upgrading all of its scanning equipment."

"They're moving toward us in a circle," Geordi said.

Picard and La Forge stood back to back. Slowly, Picard began to see the creatures: tall, long-legged bipeds that reminded him of stick figure marionettes. They moved slowly in the red wilderness, reminding Picard of ancient wooden plows struggling to furrow the ground.

"I don't think we're going to communicate with them," Captain Dalen said.

The clicking sounds grew louder and sharper.

"It's not a language," Geordi said, examining his tricorder. "At least nothing we can translate."

"Signals—very simple, primitive signals," observed Picard.

"Yes," said the Horta archaeologist Sherd. "We've got a partial interpretation: something like, 'The hunger, the hunger,' over and over. That's as close as we can come."

"It would be a hard, restricted life in this sphere," Picard said. "This may be what . . . devolved . . .

from the life forms that stayed inside. A very small population."

"And apparently a very hungry population," Captain Dalen said emphatically. "And not necessarily small. We happened upon them in the very first place we popped up, and they could be spread over an area as large as North America. And I'll give you a fair bet it's not rocks they hunger after."

Geordi increased the range on his tricorder and shook his head. "Too right, Captain Dalen. I'm beginning to worry that charcoal broiled humanity may be the flavor of choice."

"Then you should leave?"

"I think we'd better. Good safety tip."

"We'll come after you," Captain Dalen said. "If these creatures don't regard us as tasty, better to have us between them and you."

A dusty wind came up as Picard followed Geordi toward the opening in the ground. The marionettes stopped, and seemed to sway slightly. Then, as suddenly as it had come, the wind was gone.

The clicking resumed.

Picard and Geordi reached the opening and looked down. A faint light showed from the bay of the shuttle.

"You first," Picard said.

La Forge nodded, sat down on the edge, and slid away.

Picard waited, then took a last look at the desolate

landscape beneath the red dwarf. Here all hope, it seemed, had ended, and these poor devils had somehow survived to pay the price of the experiment in Dyson Sphere construction. Why had this been permitted? Why had no one thought to sweep the surface clean before abandoning it . . . ?

It occurred to him then that if these life forms had survived here, however wretchedly, then there might be others lost inside the vastness of the Dyson Sphere. He could not assume that any other beings would be any more friendly than these—and others might have some of the resources of the Sphere's builders at their command.

The circle of stick figures was closing now, like a noose.

A sudden gust of wind caught his cheek, scraping it with a burst of dust. Picard touched his face, and saw blood on his fingers.

"Hurry!" Captain Dalen called out. "They look as though they might be considering the virtues of a silicon-based diet."

Captain Picard sat down on the edge of the opening and readied to slide down, then took a last look at the dwarf sun. Something black was moving across its surface, in a fast, close orbit. As he watched, it reached the rim and disappeared.

He was out of time. The alien figures were only a few tens of meters away. He let go and slid, feet first, into the opening.

At first it was quick, then "down" became up and Picard realized that he would have to turn around to climb. He managed it after two tries, and in a few minutes was ascending through low gravity, into the brightly lit shuttle compartment.

"There's something else in there," he announced, thinking again of the catastrophe that was coming, and how little time there was to explore. A decade might not be enough merely to visit all the important places on the inner surface of the sphere he had just exited, and no one would give him decades, unless somehow the Dyson Sphere could be saved. "It's in close orbit around the red dwarf. Might be a vessel." And now he had another problem—the presence of biological life forms that might be a danger to him and the crew of the *Darwin*.

"But we'd have to get the shuttle inside," Geordi said, "which means a bigger hole. Or find another way in."

"We have to decide," Picard said, "whether to continue here or to spend our time elsewhere."

"What did it look like?" Geordi asked. "Do you suppose it was an old starship that found its way in and got stranded? Or just something the Dysons left behind?"

"Difficult to say whether it was a vessel, a small moon, or . . . or, who knows what?"

"Mostly who knows what," said Captain Dalen, as she hauled herself out of the pit. "I saw it, too. It's another sphere, Captain. About thirty-three kilometers across."

Picard frowned. "A prototype of the prototype?" he asked.

"A sphere, within a sphere, within a sphere," sang the Horta as Lieutenant Jee emerged from the tunnel. "And who knows? Is yet a smaller prototype hidden within the prototype's prototype?"

"Or another within that?" Picard wondered aloud. "And another, and another, each with its own dwarf sun and a replica of the Great Scott Sea? If we can find the first prototype, and if it is small enough to be contained in the shuttle bay of the *Enterprise,* the information we could take with us would be priceless."

"Those are very big ifs, Captain," La Forge said.

"Beautiful ifs, Geordi."

Sherd and Kodo were now exiting the tunnel. "Riker to Picard," a voice called.

"Picard here."

"Captain, we've just sighted a ship coming around the far side of the homeworld. It's in orbit, and not putting out many signs of power. But it is equipped with cryo-controlled antimatter pods. I presume it's the source of those gamma flares you detected. No signs of a subspace cooling system. It uses space itself as a dump for engine heat."

"A real museum piece, then."

"Yet brand new, in working order," Riker said,

with what sounded like admiration. "The ship's almost all engine. Payload capacity: no more than two dozen people, living in very cramped quarters."

"Can you see them?"

"The *Darwin*'s scans do confirm life forms, Captain."

Picard considered this for a moment, realizing that he was now faced with the fact of intelligent, spacefaring life that would die in the next two weeks. He wondered if they could be aware of the coming destruction. To hide from them would protect the *Darwin;* to keep at a distance from them would eliminate the risk of both conflict and cultural contamination. In the vastness of the Dyson Sphere, the life forms aboard that alien ship might simply assume that the *Darwin* and its crew were only yet more denizens of Dyson that they had not yet encountered.

But he knew that he and his human and Horta colleagues could not try to evade the unknown beings. There was too much to learn, and possibly even a chance to aid them if they were friendly. Still, he and Captain Dalen would have to be cautious.

"Picard to Riker," he said, "we're coming back to the *Darwin* immediately."

"Understood."

He looked at the tunnel—which had to be plugged before the *Balboa* pulled away, lest they create a geyser on the moon's surface and kill, a little sooner, whatever still lived near the entrance. He wished he could learn more about the troglodytes in the red wilderness—for he could not shake the nagging feeling that his and Captain Dalen's first impression of them had been as far off the mark as Captain Kirk's first impression of the Horta and their world. And what about the mini-spheres, if such existed? He wished he could think of his departure from the moon as temporary, but he knew with reasonable certainty, as the entrance was sealed and the airlock detached, that he would never set foot here again. Yet he allowed himself to risk thinking—to risk wishing—that Dyson's peculiar movements were an awakening, of sorts, and that the Sphere might somehow protect itself from the coming onslaught. If that was what was happening, then Dyson was at best putting up an imperfect defense, but Picard allowed himself the little victory of hoping in the persistence of a will to live.

Where there was life, there was hope, even if certainty was an elusive gift.

"What do you make of it?" Picard asked from the bridge of the *Darwin*.

"My guess is they've been hiding from us," Riker said from the *Enterprise*, "but have now decided to come out and show themselves."

"Or it's chance, and they can't help being seen."

"That seems most likely," Data said over the link. "We have had no indication of an overall command structure in the Dyson Sphere, no general awareness in any center of what is happening to it."

The ship on the screen was indeed all engine: two magnetic rings separated by several kilometers of tether, reminding Picard of a flying spider's web.

Suddenly faces appeared on the screen, as if someone had assembled them for a group photograph. As Picard gazed into a half dozen pairs of alien eyes, he tried to make out the nature of the staring expressions. The eyes were humanoid, set in a humanoid face that seemed vaguely feline, but with only a hint of fuzz on almond-colored skin. There was no hair, only black fuzz, neatly shaved into a skullcap, it seemed. The ears were round.

Picard asked, "Troi, can you pick up anything from them?"

"Very little, Captain, but I don't think they're either a predecessor or offshoot of the Borg."

Picard said, "I am Captain Jean-Luc Picard of the Federation starship *Enterprise*. Can you understand me?"

The faces on the screen seemed to smile, as if expecting that their picture would finally be taken. The face closest to the screen seemed confused by his words, then said, "Do you . . . know . . . our speech?"

Picard waited a moment, then said, "No, we are using a translator device. The translation may not be perfect." He identified himself again.

"It is working," Troi said, "which means the language must have some far-back link with others in the translator."

The translator rarely failed to work, Picard reminded himself, but one day it was likely to encounter a race whose language was inaccessible.

"Captain," Data said, "I see from your scans that these people carry no implants or other technological variations in their physiology. They are purely biological."

"Unusual," Riker added, "for a species with that much command of technology."

"I would like to ask a question," Picard said to the assembly on the screen. "Would you tell us some of your history?"

"History . . . ?"

"Your time before this," Picard explained, "what has happened to your people. Who are you?"

A look of what seemed to be understanding crossed the alien's face. "We call ourselves the Dooglasse," he said.

"Tell us of your . . . times," Picard said.

"We . . . of the Dooglasse . . . stand alone," the alien speaker began. "That is our way . . . whenever too many Dooglasse, some must leave . . ."

Picard realized that this meant migration to other parts of the Sphere's surface.

"Did you build your ship?" Picard asked.

"Build?"

"Where did you get the ship?" Picard asked, guessing the truth. The history of this race was lost to them. Far in the past, they had probably turned away from the great technology of the sphere, to live much like the marionettes of the red wilderness: as (presumed) troglodytes, squatters on the inner surface. But the Dooglasse inhabited a much larger surface area. Whenever populations expanded, fell into disagreement, or threatened one another with war, there would be virtually unlimited territories into which the dissidents would migrate. They had more than a couple hundred million Earth-sized territories from which to choose.

"We . . . repaired the ship," the alien speaker continued, "to go . . . home."

This was a reasonably articulate group, Picard concluded, possibly among the youngest of the dissident lineages inside Dyson. They seemed to have recently rediscovered antimatter propulsion within the great open space of the Sphere.

"Home?" Picard asked.

The alien pointed down. "This world . . . we circle . . . we believe to have been our home . . . not the great curving surface. We have been mapping that . . . whence on the great surface have you come?"

Picard realized that they believed him to belong to another group from the inner surface. The *Darwin,* the *Enterprise,* and the neutron star had arrived in time for a Dyson Renaissance of sorts, a new beginning among some of those who had come out of the Sphere's historical amnesia.

It would be best not to volunteer too much information about himself and his crewmates, for the moment. He looked back to the friendly Dooglasse on the screen and said, "We wish to meet with you . . . in a short time . . . and tell you about ourselves."

The Dooglasse speaker nodded. "Yes, perhaps on the world below. We may explore together?"

"We will hail you again in a short time," Picard said, knowing that he needed some discussion with his officers. He found himself liking the Dooglasse speaker on the screen, and it was difficult for him to believe that this life form might be one of the unchanged ancestors of the Borg. Again, the coming destruction of the sphere elicited pity in him for the races that would perish—races that no one would ever know had perished.

Q, he recalled, had once warned humanity that the universe was not for the timid, for it came with no guarantee that it would always be fair. A few years earlier in Q and Horta years, the Book of Job had warned humanity that the universe was not for the timid, for it came with no guarantee that it would ever make sense.

He raised his hand in farewell and the screen blanked; and he reminded himself again: Where there is life, there is hope—not as something that followed inevitably from the mere fact of life, but strongly from life's refusal to "go gently into that good night," as the poet said. It just wouldn't go, wherever it could. In whatever way possible it filled the niches of nature, lit up with intelligent self-awareness, and reached out to create its own niches.

Life prevailed.

"As we Horta have learned," Captain Dalen said in the *Darwin*'s small conference pit, "the prevalence of genetically compatible humanoid life in the galaxy—at least in our experience of it so far—is strong evidence that indeed one ancestral race arose, then dispersed, leaving countless colonies and centers of intelligent life behind in various solar systems . . ."

The face of Data appeared on Dalen's screen. "Perhaps it was that very dispersal," Data said over the link, "that precipitated the decline. Vulcan, Klingon, human—their cultures all seem to have cultivated an amnesia about their common origin."

"Except perhaps for a hint, here and there, in ancient religious texts," said Captain Dalen. She was about to say something else, but instead she cut the thought short, shifted her weight on the floor, and gazed at Captain Picard, who was seated on a cushion across from her. The Horta had no need of chairs or saddles for themselves in this conference room, but Picard and his two humanoid officers looked comfortable enough on their cushions. Conference screens jutted out from the floor in front of all of them. Troi, the female humanoid, leaned toward her small screen.

The captain of the *Enterprise* looked at the Horta strangely, as if he were about to shiver. He gave the image of the android on his own conference screen the same look.

"Maybe we should not think of it as a decline," Picard said. "Perhaps they thought it best to spread themselves thinly, to insure a long-term run of diversity. One might see that the peoples of the Sphere are also spread thin, in a smaller but not as beneficial version of our humanoid galactic diaspora."

"Or," Riker said from the bridge of the *Enterprise,* "maybe the galactic dispersal was an attempt to flee something, an old enemy. It may be that this Sphere is the first and last of its kind, coming into existence right at the time of a dispersal of races, perhaps even precipitating it."

Above the conference pit, a viewscreen showed the neutron star, wrapped in slowed time. It was so massive that a teaspoon of it outweighed the *Darwin* and the *Enterprise* put together; yet it was wider than most starships, and, as it spun at thousands of revolutions per second, it appeared to drag little frames of time and space after itself with the same ease that tornadoes swept up pebbles and grass.

Captain Dalen had learned that all humanoid

species, at some point in their history, had come to believe in a Great Father, or a Great Mother, who had created the universe and watched over it. She had come to regard this as a quirk unique to warm-blooded, placental species; but as she watched the screen, she observed that on opposite sides of the neutron star, identical pairs of simultaneously created gamma photons, racing away from one another at lightspeed, somehow "knew" what each was doing and simultaneously did likewise.

Captain Dalen believed in time-dragging and subspace. To believe that Troi was a psychic or that Jerusalem was a place of miracles made her feel timidly agnostic by comparison. And to believe that someone had created a world so vast that there was no hope of discovering it wholly—what did that make her? And to believe that a man had created Data in the image of man?

The Horta nodded excitedly and called across subspace to the *Enterprise:* "You and I and the Sphere, Data—we have more in common than the fact that, at one time or another, we have all seemed to be the last of our kind."

"We have all been molded from silicon," Data called back, having obviously made the connection in a microsecond. "And we were all fashioned, I presume, by carbon-based species. And, Captain Dalen, are you suggesting what I believe you are suggesting, namely that we are artifacts, all three of us?"

Picard shook his head. "Is there nothing in heaven and Earth that is not archaeology anymore?"

"Probably not," said Captain Dalen. "My theory of Horta evolution is that we originated as self-replicating mining machines. Like Data, we became self-aware. Like the Sphere, we were either abandoned by our creators, or we outlived them."

Or killed them, Dalen thought to herself, deciding not to say that aloud.

"And who might our neutron star thrower be?" Picard said. "Some fossil remnant of the Borg collective?"

"Perhaps something more alien than the Borg," Troi offered, "intelligence vastly different from the run of humanoid life. It might have seen the proliferation of humanoid genotypes and decided to prevent it."

"As you would say," Data replied from the screen, "the horse is long out of the barn, with humanoid life very widely dispersed, but this Sphere is still an eminently vulnerable target. It may also be that the old enemy no longer exists, or has vastly changed its ways, and that this is an old vengeance weapon, still working one last time."

"And who would have destroyed the old enemy?" Riker asked.

Picard had an answer at once. "Why, the Sphere-builders, I would think. The early Borg."

"So," Riker said softly, "we may have something to thank them for after all."

Dalen let out her equivalent of a sigh. "I wouldn't be so sure of that," the Horta captain said.

Captain Dalen had been called to the bridge, apparently on a routine matter. Troi and La Forge followed her from the conference pit. Picard remained on his cushion, staring at that part of the wallscreen display showing the relativistic cannonball still on course; and he watched Dyson's latest spurt of acceleration, clearly a defensive maneuver.

I wouldn't be so sure of that, the Horta had warned.

I guess we'll know soon enough, Picard told himself. Two enemies, one ancient and seemingly extinct, the other so long gone that it was archaeologically invisible, were coming suddenly to life.

An archaeologist's worst nightmare, Picard knew, was to come back from the wilderness with no results. Here, he did not worry about bringing back too few results. No. His concern here was over too great a feast of them.

5

Songe D'autumn

CAPTAIN'S LOG, STARSHIP DARWIN
   IMPACT MINUS 12 DAYS
   EGRESS MINUS 9 DAYS

*During my encounters with various human be-
ings, I have learned that a number of them
harbor a very deep fear of transporter technology, a fear not so much of death as of being left
alive in a hopelessly jumbled state. Data calls it
bad programming; but we of Janus VI all share
the same fear. Nevertheless, Federation regulations dictated that our ship be equipped with the
infernal devices.*

I'm glad for that now.

*An hour ago, Geordi La Forge modified a new
V.R. Visor to fit my head, and transported a large
probe—about the size of a walnut—some three
hundred kilometers above the sphere wall. It*

79

was, for me, like materializing in a spacesuit above the inner surface of Dyson—above that impossibly flat surface. Even from three hundred kilometers away, even through the eyes of a pebble that was speeding over deserts and rainforests at ten kilometers per second, I could see a road passing below, and a city with ship wakes going out from its harbor, and what had to be the vapor trails of high altitude, hypersonic jets. And how many more cities lie undiscovered in this country? I want to land there myself, on the great incurving yet impossibly level wall. But Captain Picard has other plans.

PICARD SAT on a cushion in the *Darwin*'s small ready room, an odd, granite chamber in the Horta hive—which had graciously been provided to him by Captain Dalen. A slab of rock, something like a table top without legs, sat on the floor to hold the small screens and controls.

It was ironic, Picard thought, that after progressing beyond the abuses of market economies, Earth's clever and humane Federation should find among the stars the ultimate corporate nightmare, the Borg, who literally incorporated anything that moved and had something to offer, and destroyed anything that did not. The Borg appreciated any good thing they encountered. He had to give them credit for that.

Presently, as he turned his attention away from the killing star to the world beneath the false moon, as he looked at the deep scans of a hauntingly beautiful city dating back more than a thousand centuries and entombed beneath a hundred meters of volcanic ash, he wondered if this was really one of the Borg's beginnings.

A full day was gone from the available thirteen before the neutron star struck, and with every passing hour decisions would be made about what should be explored, what data gathered, before his group had to abandon the Sphere. Now that they had made contact with the Dooglasse, they would also have to consider the possibility that other biological life forms still lived here, and be on guard against any that might be hostile.

Anything that could be added to the Federation's knowledge of the Borg was important enough to override other avenues of exploration. As Rome had wished to add to its knowledge of its chief rival, the north African city of Carthage, so the Federation had to expand its knowledge of the Borg, with however small increments. Clues to their ancestry, and to the ancestry of all humanoid species, might arise from the Dyson homeworld below, or they might lie somewhere in the language of the Dooglasse, buried as deeply as any physical remains.

An electronic beep at his ready room door interrupted his reverie.

"Come," Picard said.

The door opened and Troi entered. "One of the Dooglasse has offered to go down with us to the city," she said. "It's certainly worth a few hours. It's probably the oldest city in all of Dyson, and it's remarkably intact. No other area has turned up from our scans to offer any greater interest."

"Then we're going," Picard replied. "If we have time enough to explore only one square block of the homeworld, especially with the help of one of the Douglasse, this should be it."

"We have so little time here," Troi said, stating the obvious, "that one really wonders what to see first."

"One place after the other, until the little time we have runs out. Our decisions are limited, and some of them are going to be very hard."

"I know," Troi said. "What can possibly become of the Dooglasse? What can we tell them, Captain, if anything? How do you tell an entire race that they're doomed?"

Picard left his painful answer unspoken: You save them, or else you tell them nothing.

Forty Hortas were now on and inside the Dyson homeworld. Picard listened as Jee and Sherd reported that the city appeared to have been unearthed and reconstructed by no fewer than three successive civilizations—each, in its own turn, entombed by the same volcano. The youngest of those civilizations pre-dated the false moon (and by implication the Sphere itself) by more than a thousand years. It had left behind what appeared to be a restaurant, on whose flatware a set of oily finger smudges looked as if they had been placed there by a Dyson homeworlder only yesterday, although the utensils had to be at least several millennia old.

Each hour, Picard called down the same question: "And how does the excavation go now?" And always Captain Dalen gave the same reply: "Delicious. Delicious."

Picard was anxious to stand by the Horta's side. He felt as if he were being held captive aboard the *Darwin*, confined to looking out on the universe of Dyson only through large bridge screens or the ready room's deskscreens, while discussing emerging logistics problems with Data.

According to the android, Dyson's peculiar motion and the relativistic gunshot were probably the birth cries of open warfare. Warfare between titans. Data believed that the two starships might soon get caught in the crossfire and be forced at a moment's notice to ride the shockwave.

Yet because of the great distances involved, it was a shockwave that moved, from a human perspective, in slow motion. The neutron star fell toward Dyson like the minute hand of an enormous clock, though it covered more than seven Earth diameters every second. There was actually time to sightsee. Or so it seemed. Or so Picard hoped.

"We'll stay as long as we can," he said, finally. "I'm going down to the surface."

"That may not be wise," Data said from the *Enterprise*. "We may have to leave quickly, now that Dyson has become unpredictable."

"Dyson has always been unpredictable," said Picard, "by sheer definition."

"But never so unpredictable as right now."

Data was correct, Picard had to admit. Under more ordinary conditions, he would have been willing to exercise more caution. Now, however—"The clock is ticking, Data, and knowledge has to be collected quickly, or not at all."

Putting either a real trace of anxiety in his voice, or a very good imitation of it, Data now said, "I have studied your map scans of the buried city, Captain, and find that we can resolve objects as small as coins scattered on the floor of a still-unexcavated meat market."

On Picard's screen, an aerial view of the *Cousteau* and the *Engford* appeared, parked beside what appeared to be an open pit mine. "Captain Dalen's away team has exposed a town square," Data continued, "and a number of the streets are accessible as tunnels, and are quite safe. Of course, I think the Hortas and our scans will give us all we need to know . . ."

"We want to see it for ourselves," Picard replied before Data could renew his recommendation against a physical visit.

Troi glanced at her captain, and Picard knew what she was thinking: You want to see it with your own eyes, feel the ancient dust with your own two hands, incorrigible amateur archaeologist that you are. Troi did not have to say it. They both knew that she was right. The amateur's love was too often absent from the professional mind, and the hope of discovery that Picard knew within himself was one of the great pleasures of his life, to be neglected only at great peril to his mental health.

"Would you like to see this, Mr. Data?" Picard asked.

"Unnecessary, Captain. I have already gained all that I can from the scans. My interest is as great as yours, but without the feelings. I will study the scans for hidden relationships in the information."

Troi said, "We should plan for a limited visit."

"Quite right, Counselor. Say—two hours?"

"I think we can stretch it to four, Captain."

Picard frowned, thinking of the Dooglasse, and how he and his crew and the Hortas might be the only ones to remember them and to record what they could of their civilization.

"But where there is life . . ." he told himself.

As the dead city faded into view around him, Picard saw that he was materializing in a large square that had been swept, or devoured clean, of volcanic ash. Troi and La Forge stood near him, already surveying the alien site.

The Minoan-style houses stood like squat sentries, at the bottom of a freshly-hewn crater. The Horta were efficient miners; and according to Captain Dalen's theory, her people had been built that way. On every side, tunnels plunged into the walls of the pit, and on the land above, smoke from a dozen chimneys stained the otherwise clear blue evening sky. Picard realized that the Horta did not, as he had long believed, devour all the rock through which they passed. In their mining mode, much of it—no, *most* of it—was either being pressed into the tunnel walls, or vaporized and vented.

"No short-lived nucleides in the ash at all," Geordi said as he made a scan of a half-buried building. "And I'm confirming Captain Dalen's depressed radio argon levels—with near-zero on the carbon-14 scale. I'd say it's every bit as old as she says it is, but it looks like it was buried here only last week."

Picard glanced up at a row of circular windows with their wood and bronze frames still in place. They reminded him of the eyeless sockets of a skull; and he supposed that he might be standing in the square at Thera, ancient Atlantis itself, on the day Marinatos found it lying in state in its pumice shroud, and lifted the shroud, and looked underneath.

"Captain," Data called down from the *Enterprise*.

"Picard here."

"One of the Dooglasse is ready to join you. Shall I have the *Darwin* beam him down?"

"By all means, Data."

As Picard watched, a figure materialized some meters away. It was the Dooglasse who called himself Jani, the smiling spokesman. He was about five feet tall, but seemed taller. He came forward now, extending a hand.

"Captain Picard," he said, "thank you letting—join."

Was there a trace of irony in the alien's voice? This was, after all, his world, what was left of it, and he needed no permission to visit it.

"Trans . . . sporter," Jani said, "—ah!"

"I'm glad you liked it."

"Liked? Yes!"

The mind behind the pidgin speech was much sharper than it was letting on, Picard reminded himself.

"Look around?" Jani asked, gesturing.

"Of course," Picard said, "by all means."

Jani turned abruptly and headed for a group of buildings in the southern part of the square.

"I wonder what he's looking for," Geordi said.

"Troi?" Picard asked.

"My feeling," she said, "is that he is looking for something he expects to find here, yet he feels out of place, alienated. I don't get the sense that the Dooglasse are searching for anything specific. They're just hoping to find something that will tell them who they were."

They're wandering around in the remains of their history, Picard thought, trying to imagine—almost as if it might be possible to remember—who they might have been. How many other races lived in the same predicament on the inner surface of this sphere? Thousands, perhaps millions, and with enough room to be unable ever to meet and compare notes. And how much of the same might be said of humankind and the Federation? How much was hidden or hopelessly lost about human, and humanoid, galactic origins?

"Captain," Geordi said, "I'd like to take some readings in those houses to the north." He motioned toward a multi-storied building whose door, still on its hinges, seemed to have been thrown invitingly open. "Captain Dalen reports that she will have the ground floor propped up and excavated in two minutes."

"I'll go with you," Troi said.

Picard nodded. The two officers moved away, leaving Picard with the Dooglasse.

It was getting on toward sunset. Picard glanced down at the Dooglasse officer standing next to him. The alien smiled up at him uncertainly, and Picard felt even more deeply now for Jani's plight of unknowing. He could not help but feel more deeply, for there was something disturbing, on a deep instinctive level, about buildings that looked brand new, yet had last seen the light of Dyson's sun more than a tenth of a million years ago. Their vacant windows put him face to face with the fundamental triumph and tragedy of the Dyson Sphere. There was no escaping it, once he had stood under the dome of the sky and felt the ash crunching under his own feet.

Up ahead, a puff of vapor emerged through the doorway, just as Geordi and Troi reached it. There also emerged a muffled shout—as spine-chilling as it was shrill—like Horta laughter mingled with a scream.

It took Picard a full fifteen minutes to calm the Dooglasse down.

Geordi came to the open doorway and stopped; Troi halted beside him. The scream had ceased abruptly, as if cut off by the fall of a heavy blade. There was nothing to see inside, for a continuous stream of dry, dust-laden air was jetting through the entrance into Geordi's face. The blast told him that Captain Dalen must still be alive—must, in fact, still be chewing happily away.

"Captain Dalen!" Troi shouted into the dust. "Is everything all right?"

For a long time, no one answered from inside. Then the dust storm abated unexpectedly and the Horta shrieked, "Look at it! Look at it!"

"Picard here," the captain chimed in. "What do you see?"

Geordi peered inside. The Horta-flung dust was warm, thwarting his infrared sensors. He had to wait for the cloud to settle, letting daylight in through the open windows.

"It's all right, Captain," Geordi said. "I suppose we've just learned that Hortas can't speak and dig at the same time."

Shadows materialized out of the settling dust, becoming less misty and less vague with each passing second. Geordi stepped inside. And then he saw.

Columns of compressed rock supported the weight of the upper floors. Like everything else in the room, the Horta had restored them with astonishing rapidity, yet with seemingly impossible attention to detail. Had the owner of this house returned today, he would have found his chair and his table, and his single glass upon the table, exactly where he had left them a hundred thousand years ago.

But what impressed Geordi the most about the room, and made him sigh with surprise and a deep aesthetic pleasure, was his first glimpse of the frescoes on its walls. As with everything else in the city, time had stolen their beauty hardly at all, and the sudden vision of very humanlike figures, arm in arm before a great ocean, took his breath away.

"Sublime," Troi said.

Captain Dalen motioned toward a pair of bodylike mounds, heaped in a corner. Scanning, Geordi saw that they were indeed what they looked like: the remains of living humanoids. He scanned for more detail and was surprised to find, in arrays of hydrogen atoms, the intact skeletons of blood proteins remarkably similar to his own. The history written on the Homeworlders' globin genes was more human than the Dooglasse.

"Look at this," he said, showing his recordings to Troi.

She leaned forward. "Provocative," she said. "It may be that the Dooglasse diverged further from our ancestral type than we did."

"Mitochondrial Eve," Picard murmured.

Captain Dalen directed them toward a back door that opened into a Horta tunnel. Geordi saw a narrow cobblestone road, leading downward. It formed the tunnel floor, and on either side, ancient kiln-fired brick formed the tunnel walls. Geordi followed Dalen and Troi along the alleyway and came to what seemed to be a dry canal bed. Moving to the edge of the stone dock, the three looked down and saw the perfectly preserved remains of a wooden ship, its keel pitched up to face the tunnel roof.

La Forge was delighted by what his scan revealed: "Buried in its hold—what's left of a mechanically operated analogue computer! Gears. And multiple gear shifts."

"For navigation," Troi said.

"Yes!" Geordi said excitedly.

It was easy to forget, in this portal to Dyson's Bronze Age, that in the world outside, an unnavigable sea wider than Mercury's orbit was rising on the eastern horizon, and that the land on its northern shore curved upward and upward over Dyson's homeworld, and actually formed the homeworld's sky.

Nightfall came on with all the suddenness of a thunderbolt. But it was not so much a true nightfall as it was a change of lighting. Picard stood with Troi, La Forge, and the Dooglasse officer in the middle of the square and watched the strange twilight that now came to the planet. There would be no stars, Picard knew.

A very wide searchlight beam seemed to be tracking slowly down the western rim of the excavation, as if a second sun were rising in the east. At first, the light startled Picard. It was not a sister star. He knew this in a second; and a second later he wondered if something else was coming to life here, and announcing its presence. And a second later he realized that it was the brilliant reflection of the sun off the at once flat yet parabolic surface of the Great Scott Sea.

None of the Sphere's inhabitants could have ever known a night sky of stars, or even a deep night. Their mythologies, Picard surmised, might speak of lights in the sky beyond the wall of heaven, and perhaps of a blackness. Having never seen the universe for themselves, they might have speculated about whether the inner surface went on forever or whether there was something beyond, another space containing their spherical space, and then perhaps yet another . . .

Now, as this side of Homeworld turned away from

the sun, the sky was filling up from horizon to horizon with the incurving wall of the Sphere. In the west, the atmospheric glare of sunset was replaced by the wall behind the sun, shining with the misty whiteness of a thousand full moons. In that direction, Picard knew, lay the coming Ice Age. Directly overhead, according to details revealed on telescopic scans, a river wider than the Nile was long flowed all the way down the dome of heaven, yet it was completely invisible to the captain's unaided eyes, across a span of light minutes. All of the canals Data had been mapping, even an island wider than China and Europe put together, were equally invisible. A hurricane the size of the planet Jupiter, if anything like it could form up there, might go completely unnoticed on the floor of Homeworld.

Jani, the Dooglasse officer, touched Picard's hand. Picard looked down, as if at a curious child.

"You?" the Dooglasse asked. "You . . . from outside?"

"Yes," Picard said.

"Tell . . ." said the Dooglasse.

Picard did not answer at once, realizing that it would be against Federation regulations, and against the Prime Directive, to tell the Dooglasse, or any other pre-warp technology species, about the Sphere's coming end.

There could be multiple billions—no, worse: multiple trillions of people as yet undiscovered. Even without a Directive restricting Picard's role to that of a "watcher," it was beyond his powers to evacuate even the tiniest fraction of those trillions aboard *Enterprise* and *Darwin*.

He felt torn, and overwhelmed.

What if there was a way to save the Sphere? He had no idea how. But what if?

What, then, of the Prime Directive?

What, then, of regulations?

But this group had a vessel; sub-warp, to be sure— still . . . they might conceivably survive on their own. Perhaps there were others like the inquisitive Dooglasse who deserved to know as much about their world as they could absorb.

"Later," Picard said, taking in the view, "when I can speak to your whole group."

Jani seemed to accept his answer. Then, as they watched in silent wonder, a lake of amber on the distant inner surface caught the rays of the setting sun like a bronze shield, and threw the light back into space. The lake must have been wider than forty Jupiters, to blaze into such beauty. It was gone in a moment, as the angle of incident reflection with their eyes was lost.

Gone in a moment, Picard emphasized for himself. What point would there be in telling even this one Dooglasse about the universe outside? What would be accomplished? What would be saved? More puffs of smoke jetted from the old, multi-storied building—from the upper floors, this time. Captain Dalen was busy and seemingly happy.

The Horta, too, had once been pre-warp. She, too, had once lived unaware of the universe outside. But the starship captain remembered and so honored by her people had—

Had what?

Broken the chain of command? Done the right thing for the wrong reason? Or done the wrong thing for the right reason?

What would you do, old Captain Kirk? Picard asked himself. And he knew the answer at once; and Troi put a hand gently upon his arm, and a look of startled surprise crossed her face.

"The Prime Directive?" she asked.

"I believe that I'm about to interpret our orders . . . creatively, Counselor," he replied.

6

The Furnace Below,
The Firmament Above

WHEN PICARD HAD completed his presentation, the
Dooglasse sitting in front of him in the *Darwin*'s
large conference room were so silent that he could
hear the gentle rasping sound of their breathing. It
was done; he had told them everything. Now, the
Dooglasse knew that their homeworld and their star,
and the Sphere that contained them, were mere
specks in a galaxy one hundred and fifty thousand
light years wide, containing six hundred million
stars, in a universe containing at least as many
galaxies.

Picard glanced at Captain Dalen, who sat on the
floor at his side. It had been necessary to tell the
Dooglasse everything, even if that meant shattering
all of their myths and misconceptions about the

ceiling at the end of their universe. They had seemed so eager to break out of their ignorance—or their innocence—and they possessed the means to at least leave the Sphere before the neutron star arrived.

"You are," Picard said to Jani, "already somewhat acclimated to the idea of 'outside.'"

"Yes," Jani replied, "I see it, I think of outside, but—"

"What can be outside the universe?" another of the Dooglasse asked.

"Are you saying that the heavens are no more than—"

"I see a sky, and you show that I am inside a ball?"

The Dooglasse were all chattering at once; he could no longer make out their questions.

"Stop," Captain Dalen said suddenly. The Dooglasse abruptly stopped talking and leaned toward the Horta officer in unison.

"I have lived through the paradox of the outside," Dalen went on. "I myself come from a race who once lived beneath the surface of our world, believing that there could be nothing beyond it. Space was something we created as we made our tunnels and passages, not something vast outside our world that was filled with stars and galaxies. Had the human beings—the ones like this Picard—not come to my planet, we would be burrowing still and creating space and running out of space to create."

Jani made a motion with one of his arms. To

Picard, it looked as if the Dooglasse was telling Dalen to continue.

"The real universe," the Horta said, "is a finite yet unbounded sphere whose center is everywhere and whose edge is nowhere. You can move outside your Sphere, you can step outside it and view it. But no one can step outside of the much greater sphere that we call the universe."

Dalen continued to speak, telling the Dooglasse of the stars and galaxies and the true scale of what lay outside the universe of their Sphere. Even through the alien expressions, Picard could easily recognize both understanding and disbelief in their faces and subtly alien body language, convincing him even more that humankind indeed shared a distant human kinship with the Dooglasse.

Captain Dalen paused. Picard watched the audience of Dooglasse. The look that came into Jani's face, and into the faces of some of the others, was that of children who had heard a most horrific story but still wished for the story to continue. He and Dalen, Picard thought, had read to them from the true Book of Revelations, with the worst still to come.

He waited until he felt they were ready to hear the rest, until all of them were looking expectantly at him. "There is more," Picard murmured. "This is very hard for me to say, and it will be much harder for you to hear. You will have to leave the Sphere you have always thought of as your universe. You will have to travel outside of it if you are to save yourselves, because your giant Sphere—your universe—will be destroyed in eleven of our days."

They were silent for so long that he wondered if they had understood him, and then they began to talk among themselves, clearly distressed, and a mournful, keening sound came into their voices. First, they had been faced with what could only be called metaphysical dislocation, and now they had to deal with the terror of doom.

But they would be able to leave, Picard reminded himself. He had told them so, they were accepting it, and now he and Dalen would have to start working them up to constructive action as quickly as possible.

CAPTAIN'S LOG, STARSHIP ENTERPRISE
IMPACT MINUS 11 DAYS
EGRESS MINUS 8.5 DAYS

There is a question that resists resolution, yet refuses to go away: How many other races are there inside the Sphere, the uncounted thousands of them?

And on the heels of this question: How many, among those thousands, would react as well as the Dooglasse have? And is it possible to warn them all? Or even to find them?

As for the Dooglasse: in their ship and in their

bodies they carry all the evidence that is likely to be found in the time remaining of their kinship with the galaxy's humanoid past. What good this might do in humanity's future dealings with the Borg is questionable, but it is not a matter to be decided here and now.

"*Enterprise* to *Darwin,*" Data said over the subspace link.

Picard, sitting forward of Captain Dalen's bridge command station in one of the Horta saddles, answered the call. "Picard here." The captain of the *Enterprise* was holding the helmsman's position as the call came in, remembering his younger days.

"Captain, I have concluded from precise measurements of the Sphere's motion and position that, as we have suspected, it is indeed capable of dodging the neutron star."

Picard frowned. Good news, to be sure, but he could swear he heard some reservations in Data's voice.

"Now give me the bad news, Mr. Data," he said.

"In a word, Captain: *inertia.* As you know, clouds and oceans are held in place on the walls of the Sphere by independently generated subspace fields that, even during spurts of acceleration, defeat inertia and maintain the illusion of normal gravity. But the fields dissipate rapidly beyond a radius of thirty kilometers above the inner surface; and beyond that radius, inertia is winning."

Picard glanced aft at Geordi La Forge and Lieutenant Kar, who were both at the engineering station. Geordi nodded at him, as if agreeing with Data. Kar made a shivering motion that seemed to be the Horta equivalent of a nod.

Picard said, "Odd, then—that the Sphere would have the ability to move, yet be filled with fields never intended to operate outside of continental and oceanic boundaries."

"Or, at least, filled with fields that are failing to do so, Captain. Nevertheless, something is attempting to make do, trying to keep the sun in its central position as the Sphere moves, by using all the grappler beams from the portals to move the Sphere without leaving behind the sun and planetary bodies."

"Will this succeed?" Picard asked.

"Briefly, and to a very small degree, it will. There may be a few days' respite, but I doubt it will matter. As the Sphere dodges the neutron star, the central sun and its planet are accumulating an inertial lag and will eventually strike the inner surface of the sphere. There simply does not seem to be enough energy, at least in the way it is being used, to prevent it. Of course, I am projecting from current use."

"Might not the energy output increase?" Picard asked.

"Unknown, Captain. If this is an automatic system at work, it may be defective. If intelligence of some kind is at work, it may be working to correct the problem."

Utterly fantastic, Picard thought. Astrobiologists and astrophysicists, working solely from data obtained during the first encounter with the Sphere, had concluded that Dyson was the fossil remnant of an extinct culture. Now it was living and breathing and doing the impossible: It was moving the equivalent mass of two hundred light years of stars, however failingly, out of harm's way.

Dead world indeed! the captain told himself again.

And what was it that Data had suggested about *intelligence of some kind* at work, trying perhaps to fine-tune the grappler beams, trying to drag the sun and the homeworld along? Was it machine intelligence? Or was some distant descendant of the Dysons taking control? And if so, where might he hope to find them, in any of possible dozens of millions of tiny city-states strewn across Dyson's walls?

"Where do you think the control center for all this might be?" Picard asked. "Perhaps we could make . . . adjustments, or lend our assistance."

"Of course, it is doubtful we will have time to find it," Data said, and Picard nodded in agreement. If only it had been possible to bring the *Enterprise* inside, to add its great scanning power to the *Darwin*'s; but the risk was unwarranted. The *Enterprise* had to stay outside; even if the lock system could be made to work, too much would be at stake to risk trusting the gate while both ships were inside. So little time to do anything, Picard thought. If the neutron star did not destroy the sphere, its own sun would tear it apart from within. It seemed to Picard that two very old giants had come awake and resumed a family feud. And the starships, a pair of fleas crawling around on and in one of the giants, were not smart enough to leap away.

And it gets worse, Picard told himself: Imagine that they're feuding in a lake of gasoline, and each holds a loaded flare gun—wormhole technology would serve this analogy well—and then imagine that at least one of the giants is senile.

"Just a moment, Captain," Data said, "some new information is coming in. Yes, I think I know where an inertial control system for the sun might be, and it is in the logical place—orbiting the sun, very close in, three clearly artificial objects."

"Prepare to depart orbit," the Horta captain was already saying behind Picard. "Make course."

"Aye, Captain Dalen," Picard answered, setting coordinate scans for the position Data had provided. "Away team! Prepare to depart in the next five minutes. We're readying to leave orbit."

"Captain Picard," the Horta said from her command station, "shall we transport the Dooglasse from their ship back to ours once more and take them all with us?"

The question took Picard back for a moment, and he considered. There was no telling what state their ship was in. It might not have what would be required to exit the Sphere at the crucial hour.

The *Darwin* cruised sunward, laying down a wake of micro-ripples through otherwise flat spacetime as heat from the cauldron of protons striking antiprotons was dumped effortlessly into subspace. Any large, thick-walled ship not equipped with subspace heat dumps would have been reduced to an expanding ball of plasma the moment its captain ordered up impulse power.

Following slowly in the *Darwin*'s wake, falling light minutes behind, the Dooglasse engineers did not know subspace, so their ship was little more than a web of ultralight tethers, magnetic field lines, and minute shadow shields. Their matter-antimatter reaction zone burned in open space, meaning that its gamma flare was dumped effortlessly into space itself by a ship that was never intended to intercept and absorb the rays—a fact that had rendered the Dooglasse engine easily detectable on the *Darwin*'s sensors.

Jani, to Picard's mind, still seemed to be struggling with the idea that there could be something "outside" capable of destroying his entire known universe. He had turned down Picard's offer to beam his crew aboard the *Darwin,* explaining that they must travel in their own ship, which had been so long in becoming as serviceable as it was. When Picard offered to send in a team to check out and perhaps improve the ancient systems, Jani responded with apparent gratitude, but again asked that his group be left to its own resources. Picard understood their pride, and Troi had pointed out that this was a necessary form of self reliance, still growing, which the Dooglasse would need after the Sphere was gone.

Recording every neutrino, quantum fluctuation, string gyration, photon, and electron in its path, the *Darwin* detected the presence of three small objects, each about six meters across, orbiting so close to the sun that they occasionally dipped below its upper atmosphere.

Picard watched them on the viewscreen for a while. "What do you make of these . . . sun divers?" he finally asked Data over the link.

"Whiskers," Data replied. "They have tendrils no wider than a cat's whiskers; but kilometers long. Subspace mapping suggests that they are acting as transmission lines between the tractor beams and a whole array of whiskered objects circling the sun's core. I would approach cautiously, Captain."

"Understood," replied Captain Dalen from her station.

One of the objects became visible on the screen. It seemed an ancient armored thing, vaguely resembling a silvered version of the fossil cephalopod whose coiled, pearly white shell was among the few Earthly reminders Picard had chosen to decorate the *Enterprise*'s ready room. The "whiskers" emerged from the place where the cephalopod's head and tentacles ought to have been; and as Picard watched, they flashed out across two hundred and twenty subspace dimensions.

"Data?" the captain asked from his helmsman's station.

"I would say this is one of the control devices from which the attempt to steer the Sphere is coming," Data's voice replied. "Also, an attempt to drag the central sun's core along, and hence the sun itself, and its orbiting homeworld."

"And the energy to do this is being drawn from the star," Picard ventured; then, as if on cue, the whiskers gleamed even brighter through subspace. Simultaneously, the Sphere's wall added another spurt of acceleration, and the solar luminosity dimmed by one half of one percent. The screen showed five grapplers coming suddenly to life on the distant, snow-covered side of the Sphere; they flickered weakly, unable to get a firm grip on the objects—the hundreds of them—that formed a necklace around the sun's core. As they watched, the distance between the furnace and the snow widened.

Another grappler came on.

And another.

And another.

And solar luminosity dropped another quarter of one percent. Then another. And another.

"If I may posit a theory," Data said, "if the instability observed in this star when we discovered

Montgomery Scott's ship had only very recently begun—"

"Yes," Picard interrupted, "I was coming to that conclusion myself."

"Then the star must not really have been dead when we found it—or even dying, but merely awakening."

"Transmitting power to the Sphere walls?" Picard asked. "Even before we found Montgomery Scott?"

"Powering up for the dodge maneuver?"

"Perhaps so," said Picard. "In which case, Dyson truly was anticipating, somehow, the arrival of the neutron star. It knew it was about to be attacked."

"Well, there's something you don't see every day," said Captain Dalen. "Your archaeological site comes alive and starts fighting with another archaeological site."

Picard glanced back at the Horta. "But right now," he said, "the question is: Do you think we should try to approach the whiskers and correct the system's defects?"

"That might save the Sphere," Data replied, "assuming we can ever learn how the transmitters work."

Picard nodded his head, very slowly. "I know, Data. So many unheard of quantum spatial dimensions. It may take a hundred years of learning."

"Or a thousand," Captain Dalen said matter-of-factly.

"Yes," Picard said. "And in the meantime, I feel

like a Neanderthal walking into a modern-day engine room, trying to pry loose its secrets with a stone axe. A hopeless venture."

"And quite dangerous," Data reminded.

"But warranted," Captain Dalen decided, "even if the risk to the *Darwin* is large and the chance at saving the Sphere small."

"Yes, Captain," said Captain Picard.

And as the Dooglasse dropped behind, the off-center star swelled to a screenscape of fiery prominences and magnetic trenches. One of the whiskered cephalopods was crossing the sun's face, and it seemed for a moment that it was a black opening in the star, revealing the space beyond, except that no stars shone in the deep well.

"Slow ahead," Captain Dalen said. "Make parallel orbit to the station."

"Aye," Picard replied, pressing another panel on his console.

Deep within the solar corona, and down to a velocity of five hundred kilometers per second, the *Darwin* matched speed with the station, about ten kilometers off. One of its whiskers drifted a hundred meters to starboard, another approached a hundred meters to port, then held position.

"Data," Picard said to the *Enterprise*, "is it safe to let those whiskers get any closer?"

"The subspace distortions do not rise beyond a radius of two millimeters from the whiskers, unless you happen to be standing where a whisker is pointing."

"Otherwise, it should be safe," the Horta captain announced, "so long as we do not get brushed by the whiskers themselves."

"Then we'll stay. Nothing is more important, at least for the next day, than the possibility that we can adjust the inertial controls and prevent the sun from crashing through the Sphere wall."

"Kar!" Captain Dalen called. "La Forge! Are we positioned for gamma ray CAT scan?"

Lieutenant Kar shifted her body in her saddle. "I've already begun, Captain," the Horta engineer said.

"The subject is passing directly between us and the sun," Geordi added. "Sorry, Captain. It isn't working. The sun's rays just aren't strong enough for even a few of them to get through the shell. The station is either absorbing them—all of them—or deflecting them. Impossible to tell. It's all just one big data drop-out."

Picard turned and looked at Troi, who had just come onto the bridge and was now seated on the Horta captain's right.

"I had hoped we could probe it passively," Picard said, "without it detecting that it was being probed."

Troi nodded her agreement with his first plan, although it seemed to him that she might have wanted to suggest that they refrain from plans to beam Geordi's so-called "walnuts," or anything else onto or worse yet, beneath the transmitter's shell.

The Horta captain let out what seemed a deep growl. "Whiskers coming at us. All shields up full!" she shouted.

At his helmsman's position, Picard focused on the screen—gone to maximum, now, at the first sign of something approaching from outside. He plunged *Darwin*'s prow straight down; but as the whiskers on starboard and port closed above, three more whipped up from below, brushing gently past the vessel's stern, missing the hull by mere centimeters—*perhaps as much for their own protection as for ours,* Picard thought.

He had just been scanned, thoroughly scanned; he was convinced of it. This ship, and his whole body.

He knew it.

He felt it in the skip of his artificial heart.

The alien station continued its traversal of the solar face.

It suddenly went black, then flashed out blindingly white—blinding even against the brilliance of the sun. For three unendurably long seconds the *Darwin* shook from stem to stern, shook so violently that her subspace gravitic fields could not completely overcome inertia. Picard managed to look aft and saw that even Dalen was finding it impossible to steady herself in the saddle.

He saw the screen readings drop below ten percent

power as a solar flare, pointing at him like a giant accusing finger, struck the *Darwin* with planet-cracking force.

That was deliberate, Picard told himself. *No doubt of it: Dyson's off-center star was the center of its immune system, and it was responding to an irritant.*

"All decks!" Captain Dalen called out. "Damage reports."

Picard listened to the answers. Damage was minimal, but the impulse engines were laboring, and seemingly ineffectively. That accusing finger had flicked the *Darwin* out of solar orbit as if it were a gnat . . . or a microbe . . . All controls seemed locked, unable to slow or maneuver.

Picard brought up the view-forward. It showed the inner surface, more than sixty million kilometers ahead, and he realized that if the *Darwin* failed to slow, it would strike what now seemed only a distant lake, but was in reality a vast ocean some one hundred million kilometers across from shore to shore, and now only light minutes away.

Picard knew only too well that without full impulse power, the *Darwin* would reach that ocean in less than five hours.

"Can we slow?" Picard asked.

"We took a heavy blow, with thwarted force screens," Captain Dalen replied. "Repairs are proceeding, but our direction and velocity seem locked. It may be beyond repair in the time we have." Picard heard no emotion in the Horta's voice.

"Riker—Data!" Picard called out. "Did you get that?"

"Yes, Captain," Riker said.

"Data?"

"Downrange distance thirteen light seconds," Data replied. "You may have to abandon the *Darwin.*"

"No!" cried the Horta. "We will make repairs, no matter what it takes."

"There may be no time," Picard said.

"We will make time!" Captain Dalen cried out, and for an instant Picard believed, though impact on the Great Scott Sea seemed a mathematical certainty, that the Horta would indeed gain time and save the *Darwin.* She would not allow herself to doubt that until she had no alternative.

"Jee!" the Horta captain continued. "Sherd! To the engine room on the double!"

7

The Interrupted Journey

THE GREAT SCOTT SEA grew balefully on the *Darwin*'s bridge screen, sweeping up ahead like the galaxy's largest flyswatter. On the eastern shore, vast stretches of alternating desert and forest blended undetectably into a uniform greenish-brown. Picard saw that they were breaking up into tiny speckles, now. Deserts as wide as the Earth's moon were becoming visible: white dots against a background of green.

"Impact in sixteen minutes ten seconds," Data called from the *Enterprise,* and the eastern shore drifted slowly aft. "Sixteen minutes . . ."

"Slowing our descent," Captain Dalen announced from her station, "but we will not be able to slow it enough to turn away."

Beeps sounded on the bridge. Lights flashed on the panels in front of Picard. One Horta officer on the port side of the bridge slid off her saddle at one station, making a soft scraping sound as she moved across the floor, then quickly pulled herself into another saddle.

The hit from the alien sun station, Picard saw from the readings on his console, had thrown whole sectors of the *Darwin*'s control systems into chaos. Even though resetting and repairs were now commencing, they were still a labor intensive, interminable series of diagnostics, commands, and physical restructurings. The *Darwin*'s engineer, Kosh, had come to the bridge; she sat at the engineering station, murmuring instructions to the ship's computer. La Forge and Kar had rushed down to the engine room, to aid the crew there.

Full control, Picard realized, might come only within that last second separating the ship from the sea; or it might come a second too late.

As islands and great streamers of cloud cover expanded to fill the entire forward view, Picard faced up again to Data's supposition that the *Darwin* might well have to be abandoned. Anywhere near this velocity, their first contact with Dyson's atmosphere would leave no time to call out to the *Enterprise* for help. They would be dead even before they knew they were about to die. Yet he hesitated to bring the *Enterprise* in or to give the captain of the

Darwin a direct order to prepare for beam-out. As leader of the expedition to the Dyson Sphere, he had the final word, but he hesitated nonetheless. His instincts were telling him to ride this one out, to trust in Dalen and her ship.

"We're decelerating," Captain Dalen said, "but we still cannot steer."

On the screen, the Great Scott Sea was now a perfectly flat wall of water. Instruments gave the distance, but to the eye all comparisons were lost. A new chain of islands came into view and began to grow, and for a moment Picard's perspective shifted.

Was there still time, he wondered, to bring the *Enterprise* in, even if he wanted to?

"Still no steering," Captain Dalen announced, "but still decelerating."

"Check all shields!" Lieutenant Jee called out to the crew in Main Engineering. Four Horta engineers sat in pits around the engine room's master systems display console, occasionally poking at a button or panel with a rocky extrusion, as they struggled to regain control of their ship.

Geordi glanced at the wall, where lights flashed on the master situation monitor. They were in big trouble, he realized; the diagram of the *Darwin* was lit up like a Christmas tree. The steering was still out, the shields failing.

Geordi bent over the console in front of him. The

impulse engines were faltering. An alarm suddenly sounded, indicating that the *Darwin*'s matter-antimatter reaction core chamber was close to a plasma breach.

He was about to warn Jee of the danger when the Horta commanded, "Lower first section isolation door!" Main Engineering was safe for now; Geordi hoped that they would not have to activate the containment force fields to protect this station, which would drain even more power. They needed time; they could regain control only if they had a little more time to make repairs.

But there wasn't any time left. It looked as if the ship was indeed falling a second too far.

Picard asked himself if Captain Dalen was capable of taking the ship to its destruction, leaving no time for the crew to escape. The *Darwin*, an exploratory vessel, carried two smaller craft, but they were as large as small ships and carried equipment far in excess of standard shuttles. They would be enough to carry away the crew into the great space of the Sphere, and reach the lock, which would then be triggered; and the *Enterprise* would collect the emerging orphans.

Picard turned in his saddle. "Captain Dalen," he said, knowing that the shuttles had also been disabled by the attack, "repairs on the *Balboa* and the *Engford?*"

Dalen extruded a rocky digit and poked at a control panel on the side of her saddle. "I have spared all the crew I can to get the *Balboa* ready," she said, "just in case."

"Status?"

"Same as *Darwin*. She may be ready a minute earlier—two minutes at the outside—but the best answer I can give is *maybe.*"

Picard did a quick volume, mass, and consumables calculation in his head. "Cramped," he said. "very cramped. But the *Balboa* is a big enough lifeboat for all of us."

"Ah," said Dalen. "But the *Darwin* is a great big lifeboat all by herself, isn't she?"

Picard realized that the Horta was resigned to regaining control of the *Darwin*. In the time left there was little choice but to wait out the repairs.

"And the small lifepods?" he asked.

"Beyond our control," Dalen replied. "We could send personnel out in the manual eject pods, but at this speed they would not gain enough velocity to prevent falling into the Sphere's atmosphere and going plasma."

They would wait out the repairs, Picard thought.

"Riker to Picard."

"Picard here."

"Captain, since the *Darwin* is not being abandoned, what can we do to help you?"

"In a word," Picard replied, "nothing."

* * *

Troi had sensed a recklessness in Captain Dalen and the other Hortas, a willingness—almost an eagerness—to take risks. Now, sitting on the bridge, watching them monitor readings and whisper orders to one another, she sensed determination in the *Darwin*'s captain and her crew, but not fear, not even a trace of fear.

Were these beings completely fearless? she wondered. Perhaps their silicon carapaces and their long lives made them think that they were invulnerable.

Suddenly she felt something else from Captain Dalen. There was a longing inside the Horta, a longing for—what? Vivid, intense experiences to fill the rest of her extremely long life? A desire to feel the danger she faced fully, so that if she survived, the memory of her close encounter with death would make her savor the remaining centuries of her life all the more? Troi sensed all of that, and more, inside Captain Dalen, but there were still no traces of dread, and the counselor feared what might happen next.

The *Darwin* was falling toward the upper cloud decks now, still decelerating, but glowing cherry-red, as Picard and the others on the bridge waited for word from engineering.

"Engineering?" Captain Dalen asked, her voice sharp. "We must have navigational control in the next three minutes!"

"Doing our best," Lieutenant Commander Kosh said from her station, a tone of resignation in her amplified voice.

"We're working on it," Geordi's voice added from Main Engineering.

"Will we have it?" sang Captain Dalen.

"If it's possible," Kosh replied in almost a whisper.

As they waited in silence, a horizon-spanning streamer of clouds leapt up at them, boomed ions, then parted; and suddenly the ocean burst into view below.

"Twenty percent of navigational control restored!" the voice of a Horta sang out from Main Engineering.

It was not enough, but Picard suddenly knew what Dalen was going to do with it. As deceleration continued, she brought the full twenty percent of navigational power into play, raising the *Darwin*'s prow as much as possible.

Nothing happened for a moment; then a pocket of hypersonic air caught the ship from below and her hull began to quake and roar. Picard hung on to his console as his saddle shook under him; he heard a sound like that of a stone chipping against stone as a Horta on his left fell from her saddle and hit the floor. Slowly the *Darwin* levelled off some one thousand meters above the water and rode over it, still decelerating. Picard realized that no more repairs could be counted on in the next two minutes. Atmospheric drag and lift, together with deceleration, would have to serve.

"Picard to Riker."

"Riker here."

"We're going into the water."

"At what speed?"

"As slowly as possible. There's no other way to stop and make repairs."

On the forward view the ocean was rushing beneath the *Darwin* like a sheet of blue light, more quickly on the human scale than the unperceived swiftness of passage between the stars. The human eye liked comparisons, and did not believe in motion without them.

"More effort into navigation and deceleration," shouted Captain Dalen.

"Negative," a voice from Main Engineering said. "This is as slow and controlled as we'll get."

"Set us down," Captain Dalen said. "The water will slow us, if we land gently enough."

Picard braced himself, since the crew could not rely on the ship's usual inertial control—

—And the *Darwin* touched, and skipped, and touched again, shooting forward but slowing.

Picard's body wanted to continue forward in time-honored Newtonian fashion, but he had never been a man for fashion. He held himself in his saddle, knowing full well that momentum could easily be stronger than a man's grip on a physical object; but he held—

—And the ship slowed to a strong plowing motion across the water, stopped, and started to sink.

Picard knew that the vessel was not taking water; but a starship was not a submarine. It would sink until it reached equilibrium with the sea and could sink no more.

Troi hurried toward the Horta officer who had fallen to the floor, but that Horta was moving now, apparently unharmed. Captain Dalen was already getting reports from sick bay about injuries aboard ship.

"Captain Picard," Data said from the *Enterprise*, as if *Darwin*'s safe landing had never been in doubt.

"Picard here."

"The Sphere's attempts to avoid the neutron star continue badly. The central sun is failing to be pulled along by the grapplers, and is drifting toward your position, relatively speaking. If no corrections are made, and if the Sphere continues with its fits and starts of acceleration, the sun will strike the Great Scott Sea in approximately six days . . ."

"Where, exactly, will the sun set?" Picard asked.

"Right where you are standing," came the reply.

"And that will be bad, right?" the Horta captain sang.

". . . Yes," Data said hesitantly, as if confused by the black humor of the situation. "If you had managed to establish a link with one of the control stations, we might have made it possible to keep the sun out of the water."

Riker said, "I'm sending in a shuttle with Crusher, Worf, and Guinan, to give you a hand. I know you may not need it, but I want to feel better about that lock opening reliably, so here's a chance to test it again. Guinan, by the way, insisted on going, and I have a feeling she might be of use there."

"We're caring for our injured, Commander Riker," Captain Dalen replied. "Mostly mild concussions and the odd exoskeletal chip, but nothing life-threatening."

"What about your ship?"

"We're afloat now, half down in the water. I think we can make repairs and be able to lift off."

"How soon?" Riker asked.

"As soon as our programs can be rebuilt."

"You may have to leave in your shuttles," Riker said, "if the ship . . ."

"Shuttles and ship," Captain Dalen said, "are in the same state of jumbled control programs. They will be repaired at the same time. Besides, abandoning the *Darwin* is not a good idea."

"Compared to what?" Troi muttered under her breath as she returned to her station near Dalen.

"Captain Picard," Riker said, "if the *Darwin* or your shuttles can't lift, we'll have to shuttle you out."

Picard hesitated. "A day will tell what we can repair," he said, knowing full well that in the last possible resort the *Enterprise* herself would have to enter the Sphere to effect rescues. It could be done, he supposed, with shuttles standing outside to trigger the lock if necessary. He had to think ahead, to all possible outcomes, whatever the actual outcome.

And Captain Dalen, he was certain, was thinking in the same way. The Horta had seen more than a few strange outcomes in her long life.

8

Voices From the Past

THE SHUTTLECRAFT NOSED DOWN toward a chain of
little white clouds and islands sprinkled over a sea
that was flat and blue-green and impossibly vast.
Beverly Crusher gazed at the small viewscreen near
her as the specks slowly swelled in size. There was
the hiss of increasingly dense air against the hull,
and a perceptible shudder in the floor panels. The
prow nosed down another five degrees and Beverly,
tensing herself, glanced to her right, where Worf sat
at the *Feynman*'s controls.

"We will be at the *Darwin*'s side in two minutes,"
he announced.

For Riker to send Worf to help the *Darwin* made
sense; the Klingon's courage could be trusted in any
crisis. For her part, Crusher was sure that her

medical skills would be useful, even if treating Horta patients might require as much knowledge of masonry as of surgery. But Guinan's reasons for wanting to come along with them were a mystery. There was, Crusher thought, no real reason for Guinan to be here.

She turned toward the bartender, who was seated on her left. Guinan wore her usual serene, Buddha-like smile; she glanced at Crusher and nodded, as if to reassure her.

"This is truly something to see," Guinan murmured. "I didn't want to miss a chance to explore even a little bit of it," but then her eyes clouded, as if she were thinking of something else. Crusher recalled the crew's earlier speculations about the origins of the Sphere. She had dismissed the notion that ancestors of the Borg might be its builders, but now, with Guinan at her side, that possibility nagged at Crusher again.

Could that be what had driven Guinan to insist on coming with them? Maybe she was convinced that the people who had all but exterminated her species were indeed the creators of this wonder. Was she here to admire the artifact, Crusher wondered, or to rejoice in its devastation?

The *Darwin* was not quite a submarine, Picard reminded himself as he emerged through a manual service hatch and stood on top of the vessel under a cloudy sky. Engineering had finally killed all forward propulsion, so the ship was not even much of an ocean-going vessel. Standing on the hull was difficult, at best. Under the influence of the internal subspace fields, all the decks had seemed perfectly level; it was not until he actually climbed outside that Picard realized *Darwin* was angled down by the bows, nearly twenty degrees.

They were adrift near a group of islands, awaiting repairs and waiting also for Beverly Crusher, Worf, and Guinan to arrive. The sea was as calm as a quarry pool, and there was not the whisper of a breeze. But this would change, Picard knew. Bathymetric scans had shown that the sea surface was getting hotter already, progressively hotter. Unless someone, or something, in Dyson took control, the progression would continue until atoms of hydrogen and oxygen, dissociated from water, raced away from this place hotter than live steam, hotter than molten glass, hotter than aluminum composite emerging white from a furnace.

There was a clap of thunder overhead, the sonic boom of the *Feynman* as it slowed to subsonic flight. Picard watched the shuttlecraft drop through the clouds and approach his position, then gave a wave and touched his communicator.

"It is good to see you, Captain," Worf said over the comm.

"Sorry we can't let you into the shuttle bay," Picard replied, "but I think there's room to anchor up top."

"Yes, Captain, I have already programmed the landing parameters. We will just fit behind you."

Picard flagged the shuttlecraft in for final approach to the *Darwin*'s stern, and the *Feynman* crossed a small opening in the clouds, through which the vastness of the Dyson Sphere's far inner surface was partly visible—a sky of land beyond the sky, covering the sky of stars below itself—and he thought of Dylan Thomas's lines of poetry: "They shall have stars at elbow and foot . . . And death shall have no dominion." Except that death was coming to this great inward shore, threatening with two stars—the interior sun, almost at elbow, now, and the onrushing neutron star, at foot.

The shuttlecraft swooped in and hovered over the impulse engines, then settled onto the flat plain just aft of the bridge. Picard breathed deeply of the Sphere's ancient air, and went forward to greet his crewmembers.

Beverly Crusher came out first, followed by Worf and Guinan. "Captain," the physician said, moving past him toward an open hatch, "looks like I'll be getting some experience with Horta physiology after all—" and then, looking around, she added, "but, damn it all, Jean-Luc; do you always have to cut these things so close?"

"Close, Beverly? We had whole *seconds* to spare."

"Captain Picard," Worf said, "the Dyson Sphere is going from bad to worse. I think we should leave as soon as the *Darwin* is fit again, while we can do so without great difficulty."

"You may be right," Picard said, suddenly gazing past Worf to the islands in the distance, clearly visible with absolutely no fall-off beyond the horizon. This was a feature distinctive of the flattest place in the universe. But he was forced to remind himself that it was only an apparent flatness, born of the widest curved space ever built. Einstein had been forced to struggle with a similar problem while attempting to probe the even more exotic concept of spacetime curvature—meaning, the entire universe: "Most people are confused by curved space," the physicist had declared, "even those who must live in curved spaces."

Confusion. This artifact has the power to overwhelm, Picard warned himself. I must be careful. Confusion . . .

It seemed that a strange singing sound was coming from the islands, as if something were vibrating just beyond the range of his hearing . . .

He broke the spell and noticed that Guinan was watching him carefully. She walked down the slanting hull and stood beside him, and he wondered what she was thinking.

He said, "Those islands are only a random sample of what this world has to offer, by way of secrets, and probably the last such sample we'll ever have."

"We have time to see them," Guinan said softly,

as if she knew something or someone there. She seemed to be straining to listen.

"I will come along, Captain," Worf said, and Picard could not help but hear his security officer's unspoken words: "The captain of the *Enterprise* should not put himself in danger." Except that this mission was intended to involve the captain from the start, and there was nothing Worf could do except to be present and protective.

As the Klingon climbed into the cockpit of the *Feynman,* something on "those islands" beckoned to Picard, like the Sirens of Greek mythology. The still air brought strangeness, and he thought of how death had been prophesied to Odysseus—"It shall come to you out of the sea, death in his gentlest guise."

"Troi to Picard."

He touched his communicator. "Picard here."

"Dr. Crusher is assisting with the injured— mostly concussions," Troi's voice continued. "Repairs should be complete in about twelve hours, Captain Dalen estimates."

"Then we *do* have time to see the islands," Picard said. "Maybe we even have time enough to take another stab at the sun—from afar, next try, and maybe—just maybe we can change—"

Guinan put a hand to the side of his face, and something infinitely joyful yet shocking ran through him like lightning through salt water. "You will change nothing," she whispered, "except your own decided course."

"What?"

"Nothing lasts forever, Jean-Luc; not our great machines, and least of all us. Time will have its say. It always does."

"My decided course?" he said.

"Remember, they say time—"

"—Is the fire in which we burn," he finished for her, and she took her hand away from his face.

"Remember," she said again. "Remember."

Picard could not remember when he had seen a sea so calm. Worf, at the controls, skimmed the *Feynman* like a hypersonic stealth fighter over the island group, making a proud, wide arc at treetop level, then stopping abruptly in midair and climbing.

Viewed from on high, the islands were a chain of circular green patches, floating like waterlilies on a vast pond. The first island was the largest, and it now revealed a startling sight: a circle-within-circles strewn field of broken porcelain tiles, criss-crossed by bridge supports and canals. Picard checked his panel sensors and knew that his ears had been right: A high-pitched sound was rising from the ruins.

"Beautiful," Guinan said. "Like Plato's description of lost Atlantis."

"Do you somehow know this place?" Picard asked, wondering.

"No, Captain," she said, smiling. "I haven't been here before."

"Then why did you ask to come?" he said, thinking again of the intricacies of their relationship. It was one he did not fully understand; but he also felt that he did not have to understand it, now, soon, or ever. Like the Horta, Guinan could look back across centuries of life, lovers, children, and hurts—her civilization had been erased by the Borg—and yet still she looked forward with the constructive efforts that she had brought to the *Enterprise.*

"I have come," she said at last, "to help as much as I can."

As Worf set the shuttle down in a perfectly white square, Picard thought of the fragility of porcelain, and reminded himself that once shattered by the moving sun, the Sphere could not be mended. Guinan's words therefore puzzled him, because she would know better than anyone that not very much could be done for the inhabitants of Dyson. Yet she was not here simply to explore.

"I came to help," Guinan continued, "that's all."

The clouds parted when they came out of the shuttle, revealing a blazing sun and a white-surfaced city of collapsed porcelain towers and terraced pools. A breeze rose suddenly from the sea and screamed thinly through the ruins. The sun had stopped in the sky, much as the Bible said it once stopped for Joshua; and because of that miraculous paradox, that miraculous inertia, it was going to actually set—in a manner of speaking.

How to turn back the miracle?

That was the question.

Picard and Guinan came to the edge of a canal, then gazed down into water that was as blue as a steel mirror. Guinan took his arm and pulled him back from the edge. He glanced at her questioningly, then looked back in time to see a large squid-like creature rising from the smooth surface. It put out tentacles onto the white walkway, pulled itself halfway out of the water, and seemed to wait.

"Intelligent beings," Guinan said. "I felt their presence from the shuttlecraft when we were inside the Sphere."

Picard saw others darting underneath the water, some moving so swiftly that he could barely glimpse them. Calmly, he asked, "How many of these people do you suppose live here?"

"Around only these islands?"

Picard nodded.

"I don't have to suppose. I am picking it up now. Thousands. Five or six thousand."

Picard felt the muscles of his face tighten. "And how many more—across the expanse of this entire sea?"

"Billions."

"Nooo . . ."

"And that's just one race."

"I don't think the authors of the Prime Directive visualized this situation, do you?"

Guinan said nothing. This time she did not even shake her head. Like a skilled bartender, she seemed to realize that her role was to be part philosopher, part psychiatrist, and part psychic.

"I wonder if they know what will happen," Picard said.

Guinan gazed intently at the creature for a few moments. Its tentacles were moving in what looked like signals of some kind. "They know," she said, "that a great danger is coming. My sense of them is that they know something is wrong, and has been wrong for a very long time. They have been dying off for millennia. When I tell you there are a few billion of them, I'm telling you that their numbers are *down* to billions."

Picard's communicator chimed and he tapped it. Worf, calling from his post at the *Feynman,* said, "Captain, Commander Riker says we have to get the *Darwin* out of here in the next ten hours. If we cannot, he will send in more shuttlecraft, or else come in himself."

"There's still time," Picard said, feeling the sun against his face. It felt stronger than it had only a few minutes ago; but surely he was only imagining this, he decided, as the sea breeze strengthened and the clouds closed off the sun, and then the temperature dropped suddenly, soothingly. A moment later, he forgot the heat.

133

Next to him, Guinan was silent and seemingly preoccupied with the alien squid.

"Guinan?" Picard asked.

She raised a hand for silence. He waited. Finally she looked at him and said, "I've been listening to some of their stories. They have a lot to tell."

"If they can't survive," Guinan said, "it is their hope to be remembered. I'll remember them."

This then was why Guinan had come in with the *Feynman,* to remember any beings whom she found here. Nothing more, nothing less than this. It was a piece of nobility to be savored.

9

To Dream in the Sea of Sorrows

PICARD STOOD NEAR GUINAN on the south bank of the canal. The first alien squid had swum away, but another had come to rest alongside the bank and gaze up at them with its large eyes as it weaved signs with its tentacles. Guinan knelt on the bank, folding her legs under herself, never looking away from the alien.

Picard suspected that the squid was communicating with Guinan both with its tentacles and with some sort of telepathy. He could not tell if she was replying to the alien somehow or simply listening to what it had to tell her.

Two other squid darted toward them, then fled. "They had a dream," Guinan said softly, "or perhaps I should call it a hope."

Charles Pellegrino and George Zebrowski

"And what was this hope?" Picard asked.

"Space travel. It's an ancient dream for them, Jean-Luc, because they are a very ancient people, so old that their own origins, are only distant shadows lost in the past. They were old when your species was young, when my people were young. They do not even have names for themselves, or for their race."

Their silent alien companion slipped under the water and vanished. "Sea swifts," Picard said. Something about these beings reminded him of the small birds he used to see swooping over his family's vineyards in the summers. "We'll make a name of our own for them. I'll call them the sea swifts."

What they really were, and where they came from, he thought, was anybody's guess. It seemed highly doubtful that they could have evolved from the Great Scott Sea all by themselves over the course of a hundred thousand years.

"This Dyson Sphere," he said to Guinan, "is becoming more and more of a puzzle."

"Yes," she said.

"Here's one possibility. This world inside Dyson is some sort of vast cosmic zoo assembled by accident, and our sea swifts are a mere remnant—maybe pets—from one of the lost civilizations that have presumably been blundering into the Sphere ever since it was abandoned, getting trapped inside with their ships, with no way to get back out again, and therefore continuing, as it were, this great experiment."

"Pets, Jean-Luc?" Guinan asked, with a tone of amusement in her voice.

Picard smiled gently but did not reply.

Suddenly, in the distance, about twenty kilometers away, something bright and shiny broke the surface of the sea. Picard watched as the glittering object grew, swelling until it had become a new island in the chain, an island larger than the *Darwin*.

He narrowed his eyes and saw then that the new island was only the tip of the alien artifact that had so suddenly appeared. Behind its transparent walls, he could glimpse figures moving.

Guinan got to her feet and hurried toward the— should he call it a ship? Picard asked himself. He hastened after her, abruptly realizing that all of his smug assumptions about the squid people, the sea swifts, had been entirely mistaken.

CAPTAIN'S LOG, STARSHIP ENTERPRISE
        IMPACT MINUS: NO LONGER APPLICABLE
        SUNSET MINUS: 1-3 DAYS
        EGRESS: AS SOON AS POSSIBLE

The sea swifts have made an ark for themselves. That was what I saw when their ship rose from the water. They have loaded thousands of their kind inside, along with thousands of exotic animals, two-by-two, inside.

Inside of what?

The . . . "ship" was glittering and transparent and made out of glass. No. Not made out of *glass, Guinan pointed out. Grown out of glass. It had been built in the shape of a giant starfish with five thick, finger-like legs. No. Not built, Guinan reminded me. It had been grown. Like the glass spicules of certain sponges back home on Earth, or the shell of a nautilus, it had been grown. The inhabitants of the Great Scott Sea were planning their escape inside the skeleton of a giant sea creature.*

Guinan was right. They knew a great danger was coming, and had been planning, with great care, a possible escape route for at least some small number of their kind. But it became equally clear to us that their plan could not possibly work. No matter how clever their design, no matter how much thought they applied to the problem, chemical propellants just weren't powerful enough. The starfish would burn nearly a quarter of its fuel during the first fifteen seconds of flight, and though it might by that time be accelerating toward Mach-one, it would also be flying barely thirty meters above the ocean surface. A minute later (assuming it held together that long) we'd be watching its death throes, about ten kilometers overhead.

We had to tell them that their practical engineering could not overcome mathematical certainties. We had no choice. We had to.

From now on, through lift-off, Captain Dalen had decided, all of her crew and all of the personnel with Picard would stay close to the *Darwin* and on full alert status. By her decree, there would be no further exploration of the islands. She was taking no chances, with billions of desperate, rocket-capable creatures somewhere underfoot and apparently on the move.

The last of the repairs on the *Darwin* and its shuttles were completed just ahead of the 1700 dinner break, nearly three hours early. More cautious commanders, Dalen supposed as she ate her way through a mass of Federation ceramic foam flavored with a few nuggets of sand and quartz, would have applied those extra hours to an early lift-off and a windfall against the margin of error. But Picard's android officer Data and his first officer Riker had a plan for beaming clusters of pulse engines into the holds of the shuttles *Calypso* and *Nadir,* strapping tractor devices to their hulls, and sending them into Dyson uncrewed. The shuttles had become strap-on, robotic engines, hastily modified to give the starfish the added push it so desperately needed.

Captain Dalen, meanwhile, had ordered the *Darwin*'s two lowermost decks to be eaten completely hollow and flooded, providing room for no fewer than two hundred additional refugees. The upper decks would therefore become even more cramped and the water would render the ship as sluggish as an asteroid; but Captain Picard had agreed with Dalen that it was a good plan. Unfortunately, it was impossible to know what Dyson would produce tomorrow, or even during the next hour. Here,

Dalen thought as she finished her meal and emerged into one of the ship's recreation areas, a good idea could easily be ruined by surprises that made it impossible to think the whole plan through in advance. Here, she mused as she turned around to look at the new passage she had created, even the best of plans had a way of failing spectacularly.

Within an hour, aliens were filing through a submerged gangway door—two hundred and fifteen of them, filing through in utter silence.

Picard and Guinan watched from the roof of the *Darwin,* as if they were standing on a beach. "Look there, Jean-Luc," she whispered. "Do you see—circling beneath the squid?"

He followed her gaze, and alarm ran through him like shock from an overloaded phaser.

"It's—"

"It's harmless," she assured. "It won't hurt them."

But it was a dark, ominous shape—huge and winged. It crossed *Darwin*'s prow, seemingly indifferent to both the squid and the starship.

"Intelligent?" the captain asked.

"In a manner of speaking," said Guinan.

"Which means it understands the danger."

"In a manner of speaking," came the reply.

Its head was at once eaglelike and serpentlike when it broke surface, not more than fifty meters away. Then a neck, more than five meters long, followed it out of the water. The skin, gleaming and dripping, was at once like the skin of a dolphin and like the skin of a machine. Then a pair of wings followed the neck out of the water, flapping fiercely.

At first sight, Picard was certain he was viewing an animal. Then the neck had made him wonder if it might be a machine; but once its body was completely out of the water, he knew it was an animal . . . he knew this even after a jet engine roared to life under each wing and, stiffening its spine and sucking in air, the creature overflew the porcelain city, then shot through the sound barrier.

Two kilometers away, six more flying fish—he could think of no better name for them—rose from the Great Scott Sea, gathered themselves into nature's rendition of the missing man formation, and winged off in the same direction the first flier had gone.

"You were right," Guinan said. "Evolution has taken some strange turns here."

"Impossible turns," Picard said, and reminded himself again that Great Scott was only a random sample of Dyson, and probably not even the most interesting place in the Sphere.

He shook his head. Even at supersonic speed, the fish had no hope of flying to safety across light minutes of ocean, even if months remained before the sun fell out of the sky. If only he could save just one of those miraculous creatures, he thought.

"It's all degenerating into chaos and blunders," he

Charles Pellegrino and George Zebrowski

lamented. "Perhaps the biggest blunders of all time."

"If it helps you at all," Guinan said, "there will be almost no one to judge our actions; and even if there were, they would conclude that there is not much we can do with a structure of this size. We have not caused this situation."

"I wonder," Picard said, knowing that she lived as one of the last witnesses who could judge the Borg for the crime perpetrated against her people, and he wondered if justice might one day flow from her memory of what had happened. He wanted to voice, again, his suspicions about why an all-consuming neutron star should appear, just as the warp ships arrived from Federation space. Was it time for them to keep a new civilization from making use of the artifact? Or was it simply time to destroy a past they had outgrown?

"You judge yourself too harshly," said Guinan. "I've watched your so-called blunder through Dyson, and—"

"And there's nothing for me to do."

"Except what you've already been doing."

"Which is?"

"Shine a little light, Jean-Luc. Save whatever you can. Any step up from nothing is vast."

"Riker here. Are you just about ready to get the *Darwin* aloft?"

Number One, Picard thought, sounded nervous,

142

worried, and impatient. Riker's vocabulary always became more varied and colorful when he was worried. In extreme cases it became bureaucratic, as if he were falling back on his Academy training jargon. He was not there yet, Picard realized, so in Riker's judgment the situation was still potentially manageable.

The glass starfish had sailed, driven by the boosters Geordi and Riker had cobbled together from three of the *Enterprise*'s shuttles. In accordance with their instructions, the *Feynman*, stripped of life support and crammed with spare parts from the *Darwin*, was now strapped to the backs of *Nadir* and *Calypso*, providing just enough kick, according to Riker, to guarantee that the water-laden vessel could be maneuvered to a safer location—wherever that magic place, *safer*, might be.

CAPTAIN'S LOG, STARSHIP DARWIN
    SUNSET MINUS: 2 OR 3 DAYS, PROB-
    ABLY LESS
    EGRESS: ASAP

It was Commander Riker who came up with the idea of flooding the Darwin's lower decks, to provide us with additional space for evacuation of the "squid people." It seemed a good idea, but I had my doubts about Riker.

"You can trust your life to him," Picard as-

*sured me. "He's one of the best officers in
Starfleet."*

*"He is?" I wondered aloud. "I must confess
that I've had some doubts about his judgment,
having heard that he plays poker with an empath
and a card-counting android."*

*"Precisely my point," the captain said. "They
usually lose."*

WHEN SHE JOINED Picard on the bridge, Captain
Dalen had to force herself to believe what the
screens showed. Up there in the far sky, on the
Dyson homeworld, a remote probe shivered violently from side to side as a stiff breeze came up,
then weakened for a moment, then came on again
even more strongly. Its source was the southeast.
The open pit mine, with its fractured homes and
storefronts, resisted the assault of air and dust . . .
for a minute or two . . . for mere minutes, and no
more.

From the summit of the western wall, the probe
broadcast a shivering, panoramic view through subspace: a horizon on which an ember from the moon
became first a brilliant meteor, and then a fiery
sword whose blade reached all the way up to the
sky—and whence the ember had come . . . a moon-
rise unlike any other in Captain Dalen's experience,
or in anyone else's.

On the far side, completely out of view, the
erratically accelerating inner surface of Dyson had
crept up and bitten a piece out of its own prototype.

The lesser Dyson never even touched the ground, never did more than dip into the greater Dyson's stratosphere . . . but at thirty-two times the speed of sound, a mere dip was enough. The worldlet wobbled and cracked, smoldered and dragged in its orbit. After more than two hours, it was still flinging sparks and hot coals from the wound. Captain Dalen's probe showed the hull of the moon clearing the Homeworld's horizon . . . and then stopping . . . and then . . . instead of rising farther . . . it came forward and sat down on a sea located halfway between the Bronze Age city and its antipode.

Picard, seated on a saddle to the left of Captain Dalen's station, gazed at the bridge viewscreen, transfixed. The most astonishing part was the slowness—the stateliness, even—with which things were unfolding. The moon was collapsing into the world at a steady twenty kilometers per second— and it took more than a minute and a half for it to disappear. There went the spheres within the sphere, within the Sphere. There went carbon and phosphorus and sulfur: the most abundant substances in the universe realized finally as the pain and promise of living. There went the marionette people. There went spirit.

Meteors.

Meteors and shockwaves everywhere.

And a third part of the city was uprooted, and

hurled into the sea. And the waters boiled, and turned to blood. And the city was not.

The Dooglasse ship was more than two light minutes away when the moon collapsed. The aliens were flying with a Federation comlink, but without benefit of their own subspace probes. They were therefore completely mystified by the real-time transmissions between the *Enterprise* and the *Darwin*. Though the alien called Captain Dalen was describing for the alien voice named Riker a moon that had crashed and exploded, Jani's telescope revealed a moon still hovering above its world.

Then, as the seconds passed, the Dooglasse saw it, too. The horror developed exactly as the Horta alien had said it would, as if foretold by the gift of prophetic vision.

"Riker to Picard."

"Picard here," the captain said. He had moved to a station on the port side of the Horta's command pit. Troi, sitting near him, was tense with worry.

"Are you lofting yet?" Riker asked.

"Not quite ready, Number One," Picard replied. "Did you record what just happened?"

"Yes, Captain. I advise that you leave while the entrance lock is still intact. I assume it is still functioning."

"We'll know when we get there," said Picard, and he realized that by then the steadily rising tide of chaos might already have ruined the lock mechanism; and there was no other way out of the Sphere.

Inertia still held sway over the sun and the Homeworld, as another surge forward brought the inner surface closer to each. On Earth, Picard's ancestors had witnessed explosions of lava and steam powerful enough to open cracks forty kilometers long. He knew of a man in the Jordan Valley who, long before the first book of the Bible was written, had seen a mountain pitched on its side, then swallowed whole by a fissure wide enough to accommodate all the tribes of Israel. He had actually seen the man's bones where construction workers had found them, still splayed out in the disquieting pose of startled surprise. He knew of an island that had disappeared in a searing red glare—disappeared so suddenly that men and ships were converted to gas and the waters of the Mediterranean stood up like a wall . . . stood up, in places, higher than the pyramids; and he knew that these manifestations were of but trifling magnitude by comparison to the quakings and burnings that were about to burst upon Dyson.

10

Selah . . . Selah . . .

RIKER HAD ORDERED Data and the pilot on duty to bring the *Enterprise* nearly close enough to trigger the lock's external grapplers . . . almost, but not quite close enough. Closing the distance gave him seconds more of breathing space, and he supposed that seconds would make all the difference in the world, if it became necessary for him to repeat the *Jenolen* maneuver with the *Darwin,* the Dooglasse ship, and the starfish.

The starfish? Riker wondered. We're going to be cramped. It's likely to get awfully cramped in here before this is all settled.

The *Darwin* had beamed two probes to the Dyson Homeworld. The first, which dived headlong into the atmosphere, revealed nothing on the *Enterprise*'s

bridge screen, nothing except wind-driven dust illu-
minated by such incessant lightnings that they
blended undetectably into a continuous yellow glare.

The view from space was no more revealing. The
blue-green dot, with its miniature version of the
Great Scott Sea, was now a ghostly dark sphere. As
Riker watched from the captain's command station,
no snow-capped mountain, no patch of blue ocean,
shone through anywhere. The bridge was silent
except for the intermittent beeps of their equipment;
all of the officers on duty were staring at the viewscreen. Riker knew that everyone on the bridge was
now feeling inertia's threat more keenly than any
screen or sensor could convey. It hung in their
minds's sky like a hammer readying to shatter a
history.

"Selah," the voice of Captain Dalen intoned. ". . .
Will not we fear, though the mountains be
carried into the midst of the sea; though the waters
thereof roar and be troubled, though the mountains
shake with the swelling thereof. Selah . . . the world
melted . . . Selah."

The Horta captain, Riker realized, was recalling
the Forty-sixth Psalm. He caught a look of dismay
on the face of an officer at his left, then shrugged. An
alien archaeologist quoting the Book of Psalms?
Well, and why not? Nothing else on this mission had
gone as expected.

He feared the possibility of having to bring the

Enterprise inside the Sphere; yet he knew that he would do so if the lives of Picard and those with him were endangered . . . and yet he also knew that if going inside meant certain destruction for the ship and its crew, he would pull away and live with the decision as best he could. He was not a stranger to difficult decisions, even where Picard's life was involved.

On the right side of Riker's bridge screen, no voice outfeeds came from the cockpit of the *Balboa;* but he could see that Worf was double-checking and triple-checking the shuttle's controls, ready to turn the *Balboa* into a lifeboat if the *Darwin* itself failed. He knew how his old friend would take the decision that he, himself, now considered and dreaded.

The Klingon did not look up.

Worf knew that more could go wrong in this operation than could be foreseen. Even the indefatigable Data had given no new warnings. He could guess what the android was doing in this dark field tonight: running increasingly intractable probability curves, trying to predict scenarios for failure, trying to predict the unpredictable. The central disaster was beyond the resources of Klingon, or human, or human-appearing android to prevent, even if given every manner of brute strength already known to them; and the Klingon doubted that there was any technology accessible inside the Sphere that could be brought into play in time. He wondered if this time the *Enterprise* would be forced simply to stand aside and watch what happened, and his warrior's will rebelled against the thought, even as his intellect went on bended knee before the realities.

"Captain Picard," Data called across subspace, "you really should be airborne by now."

"What is it?" Picard replied from the bridge of the *Darwin*. "Has Great Scott lurched again toward the sun?"

"That too," Data's voice replied, "and something else, far less predictable. The sun is fading toward the red dwarf state. It appears to be dying, sir."

And how will Dyson's sun die? Picard thought.

"Have you been able to beam in the additional observation probes?" Data asked. "Especially the solar probes?"

"They were not a priority," Picard explained. "We've only just now gotten them away. Can you see yet?" He waited for the android's answer.

Data glanced at the forward screen and saw nothing except his own, *Enterprise*-eye view of the Sphere's outer surface: a level, airless plain that seemed endless. For an instant, he admired the complete lack of wear and tear on Dyson's skin, then cut short the amount of time devoted to the irrelevant. Sometimes, his human tendencies seemed annoying; but to be annoyed was also a human tendency. A rational being would never have even made the irrelevant observation.

"Riker to Picard," the commander said from the captain's station. "No downlink yet from your sun probe. It is—please stand by, sir."

Data watched the screen image brighten to reveal a strange star rushing up from below. Indeed, through the probe's eyes, it now ceased even to resemble a star. No longer sapphire-orange or even sapphire-pink, it glowed with the red of a ruby. Yellow spines sprang out of the corona, appallingly large, and made of plasma. The impression Data received was of a fiery sea urchin dangling in space.

"Got it!" Riker shouted from behind him.

Data checked his display and saw at once, based upon triangulations among four different probes, exactly how far off-center the central sun had been shifted; or more accurately, how much the Sphere had moved, leaving the star in place. This told him more precisely when the sun would reach the Great Scott Sea. It was "falling" faster than he had anticipated.

"Captain," Riker said, "we're getting readings that just don't make sense. The sun is transmitting enormous amounts of energy directly into the Sphere's surface." His voice was more high-pitched than usual, full of what Data recognized as urgency. "I'm looking at a scan of the grapplers, opposite the Great Scott Sea, on the ice fields. The power surges are off the grid. They've got to be fully charged by now. *More* than fully charged. But they're not doing anything!"

Riker's face was impassive, Troi noted, in the moment before he passed on a probe image to *Darwin*'s bridge screen. She saw a necklace of computer-enhanced grappler fire, burning brightly, accomplishing nothing. From their mountings atop the *Darwin*'s hull, the ship's own probes revealed nothing of the calamity happening in the world above. The sun was completely obscured by a warm haze, and because the screen automatically adjusted the lighting to changing conditions, keeping its level of illumination constant, it was only when Troi looked at the meter and scanner readings that she knew that daylight had increased its brilliance three-fold. And Data had said that the sun was shrinking, fading . . .

One of the probes panned across the face of the sun. On its surface, a yellow-white fountain appeared, a new urchin spine, a blaze that streamed out higher than the distance separating Earth from the moon. It hovered for a moment, then came out again—higher, heading purposefully toward the probe. Without any fuss at all, the probe died. Then another probe winked out. Then another.

"That's it," Picard said grimly next to her. "No hope of correcting Dyson's problem. No hope of getting anywhere near that star again."

"That is not entirely true," Data said from the *Enterprise*. "You are already too close to the star for safety."

"Warning appreciated," the Horta said, with what seemed to Troi to be deep feeling. She sensed no recklessness or fatalism in Dalen now, only grim determination.

From a great distance, a surviving probe near the Dyson Homeworld showed urchin spines flaring erratically, as if the star were signaling to any interlopers:

I KNOW WHAT I'M DOING. STAY AWAY.

Troi wondered if one or more of the civilizations infesting Dyson's walls had managed to wrest control of ancient machinery and create, by accident or by design, the illusion that Dyson and its star were alive, and suffering, and aware. Biological overtones. Superorganism. Troi could not shake off the impression—the stubborn illusion—that Dyson was alive.

As she watched, the probe panned down and across the Dyson Homeworld . . . down and across the inner membrane of Dyson. It was impossible not to look, and just as impossible not to respond irrationally to what the eyes saw. Even Data's rationality, she knew, was being assaulted and slowed. Logic dropped dead for them, dropped dead for all of them, as the sun carried the old world toward the hull.

* * *

The planet was ready, in its orbit, to be rolled onto the surface of the Sphere, Picard thought. One side of his mind warred with the other, wanting to drag him away from this place. The other side held him spellbound, for there was something fascinatingly violent and dreadfully beautiful in Dyson's agonies. The place was uplifting and utterly humiliating, horrifying and deliciously obscene. He freed himself by breaking the scene down into mathematics and physics. A mental gag order, self-imposed. It was the only way.

"Will the planet actually roll?" he asked Data. "Or do you suppose it will go through the Sphere? Can you predict what will happen?"

"I am already running simulations, Captain, but I am certain that inertia will continue to hold sway. The planet may not roll easily on the land mass."

Another view came on-screen. Racing ahead of the old world, glancing back over its shoulder as it retreated, one of the *Darwin*'s probes showed the first collisions of atmosphere against atmosphere, water against water. Here and there, microscopic shock bubbles focused hydrogen upon hydrogen and blazed forth as fusion—a billion twinkling points of fusion. Had the computer not automatically filtered out the glare, no one would have been able to see, much less understand, what happened next.

First on the upper hemisphere, then all across the old Homeworld, the atmosphere was lifted and slung forward, meaning that the planet itself was being slowed by friction, meaning that anything not solidly nailed down, including air and water and perhaps a continent or two, was being uprooted by the law of inertia, and would continue forward.

"It will roll," Data said, knowing this for a certainty now. From his station on the *Enterprise*'s bridge, he saw that the Sphere was holding up well against the old world as it scraped across desert, and forest, and lake. On the outer shell, a fierce lightning storm followed the scrape, a migrating spider's web of bolts spreading out over thousands of kilometers, and capable of electrocuting whole worlds full of people. They were the only outwardly visible sign of the impact. The concussions of light grew successively brighter as Data watched, and their westward migration slowed perceptibly.

The view from the *Darwin*'s fleeing probe confirmed for Picard that the Homeworld was indeed lagging behind, requiring the probe to depend more and more upon telescopically enhanced views, with a correspondingly decreasing resolution. But even as the view began to blur, there was much to see—almost too much to take in all at once.

As the Homeworld grazed a lake, its lower hemisphere, more and more of it, was disappearing. And ahead of that hemisphere, Picard knew, no living creatures stirred upon the lake. The forward-flung atmosphere had piled up ahead of the planet and was crashing down upon the sea, setting the very air afire. The shock front of ejected air, and water, and continental dust rolled ashore and kept on rolling toward the eyes of the probe, deforesting a supercontinent before it, too, began losing speed . . . and then the Homeworld itself came ashore. Into space was lifted a mighty whirl of fragmenting, liquefying land. From the place where Picard and Jani had viewed an alien Bronze Age city, gigatons of upthrown rock were being converted into beads of glass. They scattered across the sky like billions of glittering diamonds.

And there *were* diamonds in the sky, Picard realized. The timbers of the old boat at the bottom of the Horta tunnel, the bones in the old house—they were microdiamonds, now. And as he watched, he knew that the diamonds themselves must presently be bursting into flame and vanishing in puffs of carbon dioxide.

And he beheld a crack in the planet, a crack that ran from the lower hemisphere's contact point with Dyson's inner hull, all the way to the roof of the Homeworld's upper hemisphere. More cracks appeared as he watched. They spread out from the center of the nearer hemisphere, yawning wide and filling with fire, and appearing with such suddenness that Picard wondered if it was possible for shockwaves traveling through rock to cover so much ground so quickly.

It did not seem possible; but the old Homeworld

did not know any better, so the cracks spread and multiplied anyway, and then the very hemisphere bulged and stretched, tried to roll, and stretched again before his eyes.

"Selah . . ." Captain Dalen sang.

She called that one right, Picard told himself. Moses' miracle of the waters, Plato's lost Atlantis, John's Revelation—even these wonders were reduced to minutiae by the approach of Dyson's Homeworld. Its mantle seemed to be parting and peeling away like the skin of an orange, but it only seemed so. For it was stony and brittle. It was actually an ejecta blanket of dust and red sparks and steam. Beneath the spreading blanket, something globular and huge fell out of the world, registering, as it fell, barely perceptible but distinctive Doppler shifts on the probe's sensors.

"It is definitely rolling," Data called out from the *Enterprise.*

"What is?" Picard asked. "What's left to roll?"

"What falls away, Captain. Scans indicate a ball of nickel and iron."

"Then the world has spilled its core," Captain Dalen observed.

"Yes," said Data. "Just as the mantle shook off its atmosphere and continents, the core has now shed its mantle."

The maddening scale of events and the relentless, slow motion pace with which events seemed to be unfolding, had a hypnotic quality, even, Data admitted to himself, for him. The fleeing probe was still outpacing the globe by a wide margin. Its sensors were still piercing smoke and lava and steam, reconstructing, on the *Enterprise*'s bridge screen, a bright orange globe so vast and so real that Data could almost reach out and touch it. The metal core did not shatter as it stretched toward him across the sky. It rolled. He no longer needed the Doppler read-outs to tell him this: The globe was definitely rolling— and it seemed that it would roll through the screen and crush everyone on the bridge.

With the old Homeworld down, "sunset" was not far behind. Captain Picard was all too aware of that. For him and his Horta colleague Dalen, only considerations of survival remained—for their crew, and for the the sea swifts on E-Deck aft, who were now pulling the hatch closed behind themselves and saying good-bye to fathers and mothers and siblings and comrades for the last time.

There was no stopping the sun. All the courage and wisdom accumulated during the course of Picard's lifetime were being challenged by the onrushing mass. It humbled him with no effort at all. In the end, Picard knew, only the *Darwin*, the Dooglasse ship, and the starfish would be his concern; nothing else was possible.

After "sunset" would come Dyson's long night—a sunless abyss filled with ice. A great nobility was dying all around him, even if it had been sculpted by the ancestral Borg in the remote past; and the great tragedy within the larger tragedy was that the expedition would return home with little more than scraps of knowledge by which to read the story of Dyson's many lost worlds—if, in fact, they ever returned home.

Seconds—*minutes* after they should have left by Picard's reckoning, Captain Dalen ordered one of the surviving probes to gather the last of its power into one intensely focused scan. A fragment of planetary crust, no wider than the city of San Francisco, was tumbling end over end through void. The probe peered through rafts of molten black glass that had, only minutes before, been layers of sedimentary rock. Like blades of grass preserved in amber, the glass enclosed long, long girders: segments of a monorail system. The train was nowhere to be seen, but at one end of the system, a labyrinth of iron bars glowed white-hot.

"Jail cells?" Troi said in wonderment.

"No," said Picard, "a zoo!" And for a moment, and then for another, the captain of the *Enterprise* began to understand the Horta captain's need to finish the task at hand, to solve one puzzle before moving onto the next. The screens showed a sudden movement forward and starboard. As far as the eye could see, a thick white vapor was rising off the sea, rising only waist-high. In the direction of the islands, the vapor rose skyward in a dozen whirlwinds, and the black clouds gathering on the horizon provided a stark contrast for them. The sky, in that direction, appeared to be full of ghostly white worms.

"Now would be a good time to leave?" said the Horta.

"Another good safety tip," said Picard, as five kilometers off the starboard bow a waterspout twisted sideways and tore a hole in the canopy of cloud cover, letting brilliant red sunlight shine down, ever so briefly, on the porcelain city. It was the last these islands would ever see of the sun, until the moment it climbed down through the stratosphere and sat upon them.

11

The Fallen Sky

IT WAS HOT. Picard could almost feel the sun pressing in on him. It was an illusion, of course. Knowledge of the conditions outside the *Darwin* gave his imagination leave to insist that it was hot here—against the reality of the ship's climate-controlled bridge.

He leaned forward in his saddle at the Operations station as the Horta pilot at his right moved her fingerlike rocky extrusions over her console. As the vessel finally lifted from the ocean, kindling temperature was reached, at which point waterspouts grew into actual tornadoes and heavy swells began to form.

"Picard to Riker," Picard murmured.

"Riker here."

"We are fully operational, and rising through the atmosphere."

"Glad to hear it, Captain."

From an altitude of ten thousand kilometers, the world below became a flat white plain. Picard realized that he was staring at streamers of warm mist rising over millions of square kilometers of ocean, pushing gently—ever so gently, at first—outward and outward from the place he had just left. A hundred thousand kilometers higher, Picard thought he could distinguish the outline of the Great Scott Sea's nearer shore.

Far up the inner hull, just barely visible, was a thin scratch marking the path taken by the old world across a lake and a forest. At least, he thought it was visible, without the aid of magnification; but the longer he looked, the harder it was to see, and he began to wonder if the destruction he had witnessed in real time, through subspace channels, might not yet be visible without the probe because the light now reaching the *Darwin* from the inner surface was still several minutes old. A quick mental calculation told him that more than enough time had passed, that the scratch should be visible to him; but like so much else in Dyson, it was swallowed by Dyson's immensity.

He called up a telescopic view and . . . and there it was: The core had stretched like an egg and broken, leaving behind a yolk of gold and liquid platinum the size of Lake Superior. Behind the core, vast splashes of atmosphere were crashing back again upon the land, cooking deposits of colorless methane into clouds of black sugar. The sky, in that direction, rained caramel and microdiamonds.

Guinan had come to the bridge. She left the lift, came to his side, and stood there gazing at the viewscreen; her usual contemplative expression was replaced now by awe. "The question," she said, as if reading his thoughts, "comes down to the old sin of pride."

Picard looked at her quizzically.

"You wanted to believe we could save Dyson, that we could change its course," Guinan continued, "but that belief, no matter how well-intentioned, turns out to have been rooted in the old conceits of pride and hope. You were right to think of the *Darwin* as little more than an intruding virus here. We are saviors of nothing. The Dyson Sphere was not built for us, does not operate by our standards of right and wrong, and so long as we stay out of the way and do not become an irritating little virus, Dyson does not give a damn about us."

"I guess that shows us all where we stand," said Captain Dalen from her command station.

Picard gave her an icy stare and said, "A little to one side, I presume."

They were two million kilometers high and the bridge screen's main view was panning sideways across the sun. *It does look like a sea urchin!* Picard thought; and Captain Dalen, apparently taking Guinan's reprimand at face value—*do not become an irritating little virus*—ordered the pilot to give the sun a wide berth with the *Darwin.*

Aboard the *Enterprise,* sitting at the command station, Riker uplinked a viewfeed from the *Darwin's* main telescope. The officers on the bridge's port side cupped their hands over their eyes as bright light suddenly suffused the area.

Riker squinted at the viewscreen. The grapplers—or, rather, what he had assumed all along to have been grapplers—were still drawing energy from the sun. By now they glowed so fiercely that it was hard to imagine why they had not turned whole oceans into scalding vapor; yet the machines remained surrounded by tropical islands and rainforests that were slowly disappearing under sheets of ice and snow.

"Why is that?" Riker exclaimed. No one on the bridge, not even Data, had an answer for him.

No, he told himself silently, the figures the ship's computer was now showing him on one of his station's small screens could not be true. A deep scan of an icebound grappler revealed what had to be thousands of new holes opening into subspace. As he watched, their number doubled, then doubled again. Dimensional folding? Was that possible? Apparently so, he thought, shaking his head in disbelief as he bade farewell to the universe of Einstein, Hawking, and Cochrane.

A glance around the bridge at the other officers told him that all of them had drawn the same conclusions. A couple were gaping at the screen; others shook their heads at what the sensor readings on their consoles were telling them.

"Captain," Riker called out, "Dyson is rewriting the laws of physics before our very eyes. I suggest you come to the exit lock right away."

"Understood," said Captain Dalen. "We're coming as fast as we can."

"Where's the Dooglasse ship?" asked Picard.

"They're ahead of us," the Horta replied, "and already approaching the lock."

"And the starfish?"

"About a half light minute behind the Dooglasse."

"Good. Now—"

"The lock has its own set of grapplers," Riker called excitedly, feeling simultaneously awed and defeated. "They're behaving just as strangely as the ones on the snowfield, drawing tremendous amounts of energy from the sun and . . . Captain—the view aft—look at the sun!"

Picard found a strange and terrible beauty in the horror. The light inside Dyson was fading fast. The sun, as it shrank, flickered between red and gold, as if the Sphere were drinking in the sun's power, drinking it to extinction.

"I see, Commander Riker," Captain Dalen said from her station. "Now about the lock?"

Riker's voice replied, "The Dooglasse ship is close enough to trigger it at any moment . . ."

Troi, standing near Guinan, was watching the viewscreen intently. Picard waited with Captain Dalen and the rest of the *Darwin*'s bridge personnel for Riker's confirmation that the lock was opening; but the word did not come.

"Well, Number One?" Picard asked, keeping his voice steady.

"Negative, Captain. We have to try opening it from the outside."

On the *Enterprise*'s bridge screen, the *Darwin*'s telescope showed the Dooglasse gamma flare coming into view like a false star, eclipsing the lock. Up ahead, on the ground, perhaps six Earth diameters from the lock, another star winked on.

Grappler flare, Riker thought—or "apparent" grappler flare. It was joined, a minute later, by a whole constellation of false stars, and the sun, in response, seemed to tremble.

"It's no use!" Riker called out with dismay. "We can't get you out."

* * *

Picard was trying to think of what to do next. "It could be worse, Number One," he heard himself say, surprised at how calm his voice sounded even to him.

"It's difficult to imagine how," Captain Dalen said.

"No?" He turned in his saddle to look back at the Horta captain. "Just imagine that we are still back there, amongst those islands." Picard mused on that for a moment; an idea was coming to him. "But the more I think about it, Dalen, that could turn out to be exactly where we want to be."

"Are you mad?" the Horta captain said, her voice rising as she drew herself up in her saddle. "Are you completely out of your mind?"

Picard ignored the accusation, turning back to the viewscreen. "We must go out behind that star! We can follow the sun into the sea. It's the only way you can save your ship."

There was a pause and then finally Dalen said, "Then maybe it's time for us to be bold, Jean-Luc. I can't think of anything better to do, and I am now beginning to see the reason in your madness, so I am going to follow your advice. In fact, the more I think about it, the sorrier I am that I didn't think of your idea myself."

"Riker?" Picard asked. "Did you get that?"

"Yes, Captain, and so did the other two ships . . ." Riker fell silent.

"What is it, Number One?" Picard asked, sweeping his gaze toward the bottom of the great bowl in which a chain of islands was obscured now, before even the most powerful of the *Darwin*'s magnifiers, behind a veil of mist and storm, and the glare of a cherry-red sun, down there in the bottom.

The voice of Data came back to him: "We are calculating the time remaining until 'sunset,' and trying to take into account new surges of subspace activity."

"Where?" Picard asked.

"Everywhere," Riker's voice said. "Mostly the surges are concentrated around grappler points—and in a huge rim forming beneath the Great Scott Sea. But they're spreading everywhere, Captain."

"Geometric or arithmetic?"

"Geometric, I'm afraid."

"I see," said Picard, realizing that whatever would happen, would happen soon. It seemed to him that Dyson was bracing itself for the impact, preparing for the sun to go through.

But if such abilities existed, why not use them to *prevent* the sun from going through? It made no sense to him, and yet at the same time it made all the sense in the world: The efficiencies of man were not the efficiencies of Dyson.

"Data?" Picard asked.

"It seems, Captain, that you will have to follow the sun too closely for comfort."

"But can it be done?" Picard demanded.

"Yes—with full shields up."

"And the Dooglasse ship? And the starfish?"

"They will have to be towed behind you."

"That doesn't leave a great deal of power for shields," Riker added.

"Close," Picard said. "It's going to be close." He knew how small the chances were that his desperate plan would succeed.

"Make course!" Captain Dalen shouted, her mechanical voice filled with the glee of a child.

A very determined child, Picard thought.

"I sense them," Troi said as she listened to the alien cries. "I sense the sea swifts—trapped." Her hands clenched into fists, but there was no one to strike at, no one from whom a price might be exacted for all this suffering.

The cries came from the *Darwin*'s communicators, filling the bridge with the sound of rasping, of whistling, of voices rising to a high pitch and then falling again. A comlink was picking up the calls of the sea swifts who had remained behind in the Great Scott Sea. To Troi, they sounded like the whale songs of Earth, the calls of the sea dragons of Betazed, and the songs of birds; and yet there was an undertone in their sounds that she had never heard before. She did not know what they were saying, but the emotion in their cries was both understandable and unbearable.

"As the sun begins to plunge down," Guinan said, "Mothers are crying out to their children . . ."

Troi thought she glimpsed tears in Guinan's dark eyes.

"What are they saying?" Captain Picard asked.

Troi knew the answer to his question before Guinan replied, "I hear mother crying to child, child crying out for father, grandfather to grandchild. I hear people crying, 'I love you.'"

The cries rose sharply in pitch, then ceased abruptly. Without any warning or fuss, they simply went out, like the shutting off of a lamp.

As the details of the coming sunstrike became more clearly visible, it was hard for Picard to imagine how the *Darwin,* or anything else, would survive. Where the porcelain city had been, scalding steam was now blowing to all points of the compass, forming huge streamers. Where the streamers grazed each other at varying speeds, eddies broke off into strings of hurricanes, each wider than the Atlantic Ocean, yet microscopic at Dyson's hyperplanetary scale. The streamers themselves resembled cometary veils—which, in fact, they were. At the center of the comet, Picard knew, the porcelain towers were being roasted like dishes left too long in an oven. On distant shores, if shores still existed, torrential rains would be falling out of the veils, as if making an effort to lessen the sun's heat.

* * *

In the *Balboa*'s cockpit, Worf waited for word from the bridge, while far below, great distance and great size made the falling sun appear to be hovering over the sea, as if reluctant to make the fearsome contact. Everything in him was tense, ready for battle—or for a rapid retreat.

His aft screen showed the two refugee ships, secured by invisible magnetic "tow lines."

Back there, in the *Darwin*'s shadow, the ship of the sea swifts was a little white star sinking toward what was formerly a large turquoise blotch, long known to its inhabitants, as, simply, "the sea." A mosaic of glassy tiles—each so foamy and so light that, left alone in a field, it would have blown away on a gentle breeze—gave the ark's skin a sinister, reptilian aspect. Burned indelibly into the scales, on both her starboard and port sides, the ship displayed her name in bold red script—swept astern to give the illusion of speed. As the wind from the sun increased a hundred fold, something shivered inside the ship, and her arms flexed back, like the wings of a bird of prey descending upon an unwary target.

It was designed to do that! Worf realized, and something in him warmed at a sight that reminded him a little of the movements of those most admirable and beautiful examples of Earth's avian species, the hawks and falcons and eagles. At first glance, the thing they had called a "starfish" looked nothing at all like a spaceworthy vehicle—yet there it was, transformed into an alien raptor worthy of space.

A beep from a console near his arm warned him that the solar wind, as it hissed past the *Darwin*'s magnetic field envelope, was increasing *another* hundred fold. On the descending sun, three brilliant white fountains—sea urchin spines—had swung suddenly in the same direction. They were pointing directly at him, like searchlight beams converging.

Suddenly Worf was aware that someone was entering the shuttlecraft from behind him. His hand reflexively darted toward his phaser as he swung around in his seat.

Deanna Troi had come aboard the *Balboa*. "It's seen us," Troi said as she came toward him, followed by Guinan. Beverly Crusher and Geordi La Forge were behind them, climbing down from the *Darwin* into the *Balboa*'s hold.

"What are you doing here?" the Klingon demanded.

"Captains Dalen and Picard ordered us to go below," said Troi. "Just in case," she added absently.

Worf noticed that they were all transfixed—Troi, Guinan, Crusher, and Geordi—all held captive by the sun's approach to the Sphere's inner surface. He turned back to his screen. On the *Darwin*-facing hemisphere of the solar urchin, a dozen more spines were moving slowly into position, sweeping their gaze toward *Darwin*, like the eyes of Argus come awake.

* * *

On the bridge, Picard understood that the sun stations, when they had swatted at the *Darwin* once before, must have retained a memory of the ship's configuration, much as human blood cells retain a memory of every new virus's configuration, in case they should encounter it again.

It recognizes us! he thought, just before the force of the blast turned the aft wall suddenly into the floor; and the floor and ceiling into walls.

Captain Dalen struck the aft "floor" with a sickening thud, and Picard pounded down with a wet snap that told him his wrist was fractured. As he struggled to his feet and stood on the wall, the *Darwin*'s computer realigned the gravitic field with such lightning efficiency that Picard immediately fell upon his face, coming down hard enough to break his nose.

It could easily have been a lot worse, he realized. The Horta crewmember near him had just missed his head by a margin measurable in gnat's breaths.

"Out of here!" Dalen called. "Everybody out of here!"

There followed a confusion of shuffling Horta bodies, some obeying and leaving, others coming forward.

On the screen, more sun-fountains were taking aim. Many more. Yet Picard did not move. Would not move.

"Abandon ship, Jean-Luc," the Horta captain said. "That's an order."

"You, too," Picard demanded.

"No. You wouldn't abandon your ship, would you? I won't abandon mine. I am not finished, here."

"Nor I."

"Yes, you are!" the Horta shouted, and the bridge screen began to fill the room with a yellow-white glow. "I know you," she continued in a softer tone, "and you have another destiny. Now leave."

Dalen was right. This was her ship and her command; he had done everything he could to help her, and would only be another problem distracting her if he remained aboard. Now his duty was to his own ship and crew.

"You gave us a plan that just might work," Dalen went on. "In fact, I'm betting that it will. Time for you and your people to get out of here and give us a chance to put it to the test."

"Bonne chance, Captain Dalen," Picard said as he moved past her toward the lift.

A lifetime later, the shuttlecraft *Balboa,* in accordance with both Captain Dalen's and Captain Picard's orders, was away, with Worf as pilot. A second later, the *Engford*—filled with water and piloted by refugees—detached from the *Darwin;* but when Picard looked back, he saw that the second shuttle was staying too close to the Horta ship, like a faithful pet that refused to leave.

It was all part of some great ballet being put on by Dyson's *impresarios*—except that no one had told anyone who was to dance and who was to be the audience. Anyone could be forced to watch or dance at a moment's notice as the great *pas de deux* of sun and inner surface threatened.

"Darwin to *Engford,"* Captain Dalen called, pressing herself against the saddle at her captain's station, "away all boats! Impulse power! *Engford,* you are to—"

She never finished the order. The ships were ripped from their paths, and seared, and strewn about in a concussion of heat and light; and the *Darwin* was in the center of the concussion.

The Horta saw something and tried to speak; but then, of course, she could not, and her ship was falling . . .

Falling . . .

Falling . . .

The starfish had been flung ahead of the *Balboa,* to judge from the views being transmitted on the comlinks. Picard, watching the images, could see that its captain was alternately thrusting forward and braking, trying to gain control of the ark. Oddly, it became a graceful motion to watch. The ocean, some two million kilometers below the starfish, was vaporizing in apparent silence. Nearer the red star, far away to starboard, both atmosphere and water had been hurled away completely. The porcelain city and the archipelagos, what was left of them, stood now in a vacuum on bare ocean bottom. They stood deep within the corona of Dyson's sun.

Riker listened to the voices from the captain's command station on the bridge of the *Enterprise*.

"Darwin!" the *Enterprise* called across the void. "Captain Dalen, can you hear us?"

"Balboa to *Darwin!"* Picard called. "Captain Dalen. Please respond."

"This is Jani. We are moving through the position last occupied by your vessel called the *Darwin.* There is no sign, we regret to tell."

The comlink from the Dooglasse ship showed the sun lashing out at a distant target, producing another concussion of light.

"I think that was Captain Dalen's ship," Picard said.

"I'm afraid so," said Riker, and then, on the Sphere below him, a bright spot appeared. There was hardly time for Riker to take note of it, the event happened so fast. All in one part of a second, a small piece of Dyson's shell glowed, then the glow expanded, became deep red at first, then yellower, then whiter, and then faded again to deep red, still within that part of a second.

The sun burned through with a flash.

It never actually touched the Sphere. Dyson's shell merely liquefied, then vaporized, then parted and blew away.

Someone behind Riker let out a cry. Riker sat stunned, unable for a moment to think or feel.

"Impossible!" one of the officers at the bridge engineering station aft was saying. "Just impossible!"

But there it was, on Riker's own forward viewscreen. The only view more incredible than the sun eating its way into space was the scene coming to him from the starfish.

As if somehow parachuting down through the vacuum, the still-out-of-control ark was hovering, at what appeared to be merely mountaintop altitude, over a storm that reached from flat horizon to flat horizon. Millions of kilometers ahead, where the sun had set, a pillar of fire rose from the maelstrom and pointed straight into the sky.

This was no ordinary fire, Riker knew. It was air and water falling through the hole, first yanked irresistibly after the sinking sun's gravity, then blasted back inside the Sphere. Sheets of cooling steam and ionized gas and glittering flakes of snow caught the last rays of the fallen star and threw them to the walls of Dyson, which were bright enough to navigate by. The starfish-eye-view showed rips in the cloud cover, through which whitecaps a hundred times higher than Everest shone—no, not white-

caps, Riker realized: *rapids*. Everything in the Great
Scott Sea—water, air, and over there a whole
island—was being drawn toward the crater.

The starfish, though high above what passed for
Dyson's ionosphere, was also being dragged slowly
sunward. During the final moments before burn-
through, a thin canopy of ionized gas had been
hurled into space, hurled at an impossible angle,
high over the shores of the Great Scott Sea. Now the
starfish, its engines apparently under only partial
control, was being carried down by streamers of
sunward-bound gas, as a balloon is carried by the jet
stream.

Riker feared that it would end for them soon, with
their ark dashed upon the rapids. As the seconds
passed into minutes, he *knew* it would end that way,
and then Data turned toward him for a moment.

"The rapids themselves appear to be dying, sir"
Data said to him before turning back to the screen.

Riker saw that something was rising in the ark's
path, rising higher than the water, higher than the
air.

"Impossible!" Riker said, echoing the engineering
officer.

"Apparently so," Data said from his station, "but
nonetheless it is happening."

"Enterprise to *Balboa,* what do you see?" Riker
asked.

At Worf's bidding the shuttle showed him a different perspective from the starfish: higher and looking straight down on the hole's west rim.

Worf had caught sight of the Dooglasse ship caught in a swirl of crystallizing vapor, struggling to maneuver through a snowstorm in space, but it was now shielded within the *Balboa*'s force field and magnetic cocoon. "Dyson's Spear," as he was already calling that comet in his mind, pointed back through the disintegrating waterfalls, back through the hole in the Sphere, with the cocoon of two ships buried in its tail. Hydrogen, oxygen, silicon, and carbon, stripped of their electrons, swept past *Balboa*'s bow at a significant fraction of lightspeed. The ship's magnetic field envelope shunted the charged nuclei and electrons to either side, much as the prow of a boat shunts water to port and starboard.

Worf knew that he was unlikely to see such a sight ever again; yet even the cometary spear was a mere detail in Dyson's vast and violent war dance.

"Riker to Picard," Riker's voice said. "Please report."

La Forge glanced at Picard, sitting next to him in the *Cousteau*.

"We're seeing teeth down there," Troi answered for the captain. "A whole mountain range, rising like teeth out of the sea floor . . . thirty kilometers high, now. It's damming the rapids."

Mountains? Geordi wondered, peering at his instruments. How? Dyson's powers-that-be had failed to move their sun. How, then, had they managed to plow so much mass into mountain ranges so quickly? And then he guessed that force fields covered with mud and water would look much like mountains.

Hollow mountains.

It seemed as good an explanation as any, except that his instruments were showing—what had Data called it? Dimensional folding?

Whatever it was, it was now manifesting along the entire hull of Dyson. Geordi could no longer be certain of what his scans were showing, because the multiple thousands of subspace microverses manifesting up, down, starboard, port, forward, and aft were beyond measure. Soon, Dyson would be completely invisible to his scans. From his engineer's perspective, the Sphere was about to drop out of the universe.

He was beginning to suspect that Dyson's powers-that-be were quite insane. He glanced at Worf next to him, but the Klingon was a stone figure.

"Picard to Riker!" Picard's voice said.

"Riker here, Captain."

"Where is the neutron star? Still on the same course, I presume?"

"Still on trajectory, Captain," Riker said, sounding, to himself, less awed than he felt. Then, after a long silence, he added, "As last predicted, it has missed the Sphere."

Yet another miracle, he thought, in a string of miracle-moments that numbed the mind's ability to absorb. Riker wondered then if the Dyson Sphere had altered his capacity to ever be surprised by anything again.

The neutron star missed? Impossible, Picard thought. Like everything else about Dyson, it seemed impossible: For all the effort on the part of those who had sent it, they had missed! The images transmitted from the *Enterprise* showed the neutron star moving away, clearly unable to compensate for the Sphere's last-minute maneuvering.

Ahead of the *Balboa,* cometary streamers were still gushing up through the hole. Picard stared at a bright foaming mass of what looked like waves breaking at the foothills of a mountain range. The breakers had to be utterly huge to be seen across the gulf that separated him from the shore, and yet the distance was shrinking before impulse velocity. He swung one of the *Balboa*'s scopes aft, toward the Dooglasse ship, where Jani and his crew would be looking around in bewilderment, and perhaps in terror, at a world that was darkening rapidly. Night was falling for the first time in their history, but no stars were coming out to light the darkness, except for the grappler flares, visible only in computer-enhanced green, and now becoming invisible altogether.

* * *

Geordi saw that the starfish's engines, too, were becoming invisible, though the ark appeared to be gaining control now, as it made headway against the ionosphere's current. His scans from the *Balboa* showed the starfish descending toward an old river delta before its engine signature gave him—for want of a better explanation—the illusion of folding into subspace and winking out.

The engineer was certain that a sufficiently powerful telescopic view would allow him to see the starfish, still out there somewhere, still in the visible wavelengths of light, still moving under its own power—but there was no time for collecting more pieces of the Dyson jigsaw. The wide course correction Worf was making to avoid an uprushing snowstorm—one of Dyson's reefs—took all of Geordi's attention from the starfish, and suddenly the edge of the mountain range was flying toward him, threatening to swallow the *Balboa*. The rim seemed closer than it ought to have been, given Worf's piloting skills. It was as if . . . as if the opening were contracting.

Geordi tore his gaze away from the mountains— on one side the night surf, on the other side a deep well with a comet stuck in it—long enough to take a glance at his altimeter. It showed nothing—nothing sensible, at least. According to *Balboa*'s instrumentation, Dyson no longer existed.

The instrumentation of his own senses and his own common sense told him otherwise, of course, as the *Balboa* and its cocoon plunged through the ionosphere and the view in all directions was diminished by a yellow glare.

The ring of hollow mountains looked real enough, even through the glare of ions against the *Balboa*'s shields; real enough, and spine chillingly close.

Worf was thrusting hard to starboard, swinging the sun directly into the *Balboa*'s path, and still the cliffs looked as if they were about to scrape the port side. They were covered in a glaze of ice chips and accelerated hydrogen, and the *Balboa* shot by too quickly to record even a single snapshot of the black shapes that struggled on a crack in the glaze. They were the size of elephants, the shape of dust mites, faster than cheetahs, and smarter than Data. Like an army of corpuscles gathered at a flesh wound, they spun a fibrous scab that was partly webbing and partly their own bodies. Of this army, only one member recorded the passage of the cocoon. It took notice that the two ships inside appeared to be growing, filed this fact away for future reference, and returned its attention to more important concerns.

Two-tenths of a second later, Worf was piloting in open daylight. In another six-tenths of a second he had swung the *Balboa* ninety degrees to port and, while preserving all of his forward momentum, was vectoring away from the sun as hard as he could without wrenching the towed Dooglasse ship apart.

Twelve seconds after that he looked around and saw the outer shell of Dyson, as clear and bright as high noon. He breathed a sigh of satisfaction, feeling as gratified as if he had defeated an enemy in hand-to-hand combat, just as Data said from the *Enterprise*, "The Sphere is slowing."

"Slowing?" Picard asked.

"It has stopped," Data added.

Worf gazed at the horizon in awe, thinking of the control of mass and inertia involved in stopping such a large object.

"It is now reversing its motion," Data's voice said without emphasis.

Worf muttered a curse and vectored the engines elsewhere, lest the horizon rush up to meet him.

Caught between the sun and the ground—again; but vectoring, this time, far beyond the reach of the urchin spines, the *Balboa* flew onward. Picard shook his head in wonder and exhaustion and sat back at his station, feeling suddenly unnecessary and insignificant. Down there, on the other side of the shell, most of an ocean had been lost . . . and a world as old as Earth . . . and its moon . . . and whatever lands they had bowled across . . . and no fewer than two races had probably perished.

He had tried to prevent this damage, but to the Dyson Sphere, it all added up to barely more than a bad scrape. The superplanet, having bled a little, was bandaging up now and moving on at its own super-planetary scale.

Hortas. Sea swifts. Marionettes.

Try as he might, what Picard was certain he would never forget, what he would never escape, was the realization that Dyson took no notice of them.

12

Dyson's Web

"RIKER TO DALEN, please come in."

"Darwin, this is *Balboa. Darwin, Darwin,* we have made safe exit. Repeat, this is the *Balboa,* answer if you can hear me."

Captain Dalen heard the hailings from the *Enterprise* and the *Balboa,* but she did not respond. She had sent her last message just a few moments ago.

The message was: "Thanks for the good advice, Jean-Luc."

No Federation here—not now, not ever—forever. No one was going to assign her to a new site before her exploration here was complete. The *Darwin* had come down on water—again; And this time she was down for the long haul. This time, the sun had seen to it that her ship would never fly again.

All well and fine, the Horta captain decided. It would take forever to visit all of Dyson's unexplored shores; and by practical human standards, she and her crew really did have forever.

And—oh, the wonders that lay ahead!

"It's very close now, Captain." Lieutenant Jee was speaking, who was at present assisting three other squid with the lashing of the shuttlecraft *Engford* to the *Darwin*'s starboard hull. One of the Great Scott Sea survivors had taken Jee's name, and another had taken Ensign Lenn's, and another Lieutenant Veere's, presumably as a sign of gratitude for their help.

Before the lines between the *Engford* and the *Darwin* were secured, sunrise erupted through the same well the sun had dug and fallen into more than a hundred million kilometers downstream. The star rose swiftly, returning in triumph to flood with light the vast realm it had so recently abandoned. In only two minutes, it was clear of the well, lofting like a brilliant balloon, its dawn banishing the cometary veils. Twenty minutes later, it might have been midmorning. Two hours after that, it might have been noon.

Captain Dalen was nagged by an impression, for no reason that she was logically or rationally aware, that the changes occurring outside were even more dramatic. She felt—she *knew*—that the humans would be shut off from her till the end of time; and she found herself thinking that all the universe was shifting . . . swelling . . . all of it except right here!

Nightfall had come again to the Dooglasse, whose ship was now joined to the *Balboa,* inside the *Enterprise*'s protective cocoon.

"It's still shrinking," Riker called excitedly.

As indeed it was, Picard saw as the *Enterprise* stood off and watched. For the first time, the Dyson Sphere really did look like a planet. It was as small as Earth now; and growing smaller with each passing second. The instruments suggested that it did not exist at all, except visually and as faint distortions in the geometry of spacetime.

Riker shook his head. "Captain, it should have more gravitational compaction than a neutron star by now."

"I know," Picard said, "and by the time it's down to the *Enterprise*'s size, whole Earth masses will be compressed into spaces smaller than golf balls. It should be a black hole, by then."

"But I'll wager it won't be," Riker said with a faint smile.

Picard nodded. "I begin to think we've been oversimplifying things here, don't you?"

Riker shrugged. "What else can we say? Everything we know tells us there's a whole sun down there, whole star systems full of suns if we count all the mass from which they built it—and yet at

Dyson's surface I'm registering less than one-sixth Earth gravity. The only rational explanation is that Dyson doesn't quite exist in our universe any more. And that isn't quite rational."

"Yet it is extraordinary," Picard muttered under his breath, as a fuller realization of what had happened came into his mind.

But Data was ahead of him. "Captain," the android said, "did we wake the Sphere's artifical intelligence to all this action?"

For once, Picard knew that he was ahead of Data. "We might have been entirely superfluous. In fact, we might even have been a slight impediment."

"Do you think so, Captain?" asked Data.

"It's entirely likely," Picard said.

"Entirely likely means yes, does it not, since the word 'entirely' takes all doubt away from the word 'likely.' "

"Quite right," Picard said, gazing at the telescopic view of Dyson's shrinking disk.

"Then are you suggesting that we should have stayed away, since we were not needed?"

Picard rebelled at the thought and said, "Data, I wouldn't have missed this for anything."

"Thanks for the good advice, Jean-Luc." He thought again of Captain Dalen's last message, and wondered if this universe would ever see her and her crew again.

The Sphere was a distant gray bead now, contracting faster and faster through that ghostly hole it had dug in the cosmos—and preparing, no doubt, to pull the hole in after itself. No doubt, it would also pull a part of Picard down with it, as it folded into microverses and tapped energies that could only be guessed at.

"Be careful what you wish for . . ." his mother had warned.

Well, he had gotten more than he wished for, as he hoped and yet he also dreaded that he would ever again find something as mysterious and horrifying, as wonderful and as belittling as the Dyson Sphere. This seemed to him so entirely unlikely that he returned the hope and the dread, for now, to that place of dearest wishes that waited in his archaeologist's heart. He would visit those wishes again, as surely as his blood visited the ventricles of his engineered heart.

"It has gone quantum," Data announced. "Dyson's gravitational field is . . . virtually non-existent."

Quantum. Smaller than any of the blood cells that flowed in his veins . . . smaller than a virus particle—Dyson, the whole thing . . . smaller than the diameter of a proton. Picard hunched slightly forward in his station, with his arms folded across his chest, as if he were trying to keep warm. And there was a coldness in him, a chill born of the realization that the greatest object ever constructed had just sunk from view, leaving him adrift in unfulfilled expectations. Adrift, alone, abandoned?

No, he told himself. He was adrift, but not alone. Something was out there, and it was coming his way.

And it knew his name.

Locutus . . .

"Data?"

"Captain, there is a Borg vessel at the limits of our sensor range."

So, it was not over yet.

"What's it doing?" Picard asked.

"Nothing at all, Captain."

Picard sat back and considered, then gazed at Riker. Number One was wearing his cautious, annoyed look. "Perhaps all of our assumptions were not wrong after all," Riker said.

Picard found himself agreeing, in a way: "Relativity and dimensional folding aside, I'd say even a clock that isn't running would have to be right twice a day."

Riker shook his head. "Thanks, Captain."

Picard watched Data put an enhanced view on the screen, showing an ever so faint optical distortion in the place where Dyson's center had been.

"I'm thinking about the assumption we came to when the neutron star first appeared," Riker continued, "about how some distant remnant of the Dyson engineers—perhaps the Borg—might have been trying to destroy something in its past that could be of benefit to us. Something in the Sphere."

"Whatever it was," Picard said, "we didn't find it."

As he spoke, the Borg cube disappeared in a wash of subspace distortion. Either it had been destroyed somehow, or it had sped off in a hurry, fleeing faster than any Borg ship had hitherto been clocked. Simultaneously, the tiny distortion on Data's display finally pulled the hole in behind itself. The Sphere had left no footprints, quantum or otherwise; but Picard could not shake the feeling, the deep instinctive knowing, that the Borg had disturbed a sleeping tiger . . . and it was now following them.

It might very well be very far from over, he thought. But of one thing he was certain: The Sphere's example—its future significance for Federation thinking—would not be easily exhausted. It represented what was "merely" an early, perhaps even sinful attempt at cosmic engineering, an extravagant effort by an intelligent species to change the face of the cosmos. The human mind, so recently out of its cradle, still boggled at the idea of remaking a galaxy, or an entire universe, nearer to its heart's desire. Against human wishes, the universe might very well be a "sorry scheme," as the poet said; but human desires were still too vague to know what to want. Knowledge, love, a graceful life? But when the day of self-knowledge arrived . . . what then?

And for a moment Picard feared the wishes that waited to conflict with those of humankind.

Epilogue

The Fabulous Riverboat

CAPTAIN DALEN OPENED the aft hatch and tractored onto the roof of the *Darwin*. A dozen of her crew had gone out ahead of her. They stared at the *Engford,* the sky, the sea, the beings the humans had named the sea swifts. They let the sun warm their hard backs. They breathed deep of Dyson's air.

The air . . . the water . . . the Horta captain tried to form for herself an estimate of how many days, or weeks, the shockwaves from the old world and the Great Scott Sea would take to reach her from various distances in the Sphere, and whether or not they would have, by that time, diminished to little more than loud bangs.

She stiffened, reluctant to dwell on the question,

but drawn irresistibly to finishing the calculation, once she had begun it.

Then into her icy black veins flowed blood. She had arrived at an answer: the blast from the Great Scott Sea, dissipating across a radius of more than one hundred million kilometers—more than five minutes away at the speed of light, vastly longer at the mere speed of sound—would arrive as a long, rumbling roar, bringing winds gusting up to ninety kilometers per hour. They would gust for six days; but the *Darwin* had already endured far worse, she told herself. *It means that we will live!*

"What lake is this?" asked Lieutenant Jee. "What sea?"

"No lake, no sea," Captain Dalen said thoughtfully. "It's a river whose west bank lies more than fifteen hundred kilometers to starboard, and whose delta is a hundred million klicks astern. You'll find its source another hundred million in the opposite direction."

"Then, it could take lifetimes to find all the hidden coasts, all the people."

"Horta lifetimes," the captain said, and felt the warmth within her that was the Horta equivalent of a smile. She looked downstream, down a stream longer than the distance between most planets, and she contemplated the feeling that the universe outside had been swelling, just before the *Balboa* and the *Enterprise* disappeared. She wondered what "quantum dimensional folds" and "baby universes"

really meant, and realized that she already knew. She and everything around her was smaller than a virus, smaller than a proton, and more ghostly than a neutrino . . . from a certain point of view . . .

"So much to see," she continued. "So much to *do.*"

"I want to see the place where the old world rolled," Jee sang excitedly. "What must the land look like there?"

"I believe we will be able to find out," said Captain Dalen. "I have been reviewing the maps, and I have found that one of this river's tributaries feeds from the lake over which the planet slid."

"And the hole in the Great Scott Sea?" Jee asked. "What must it look like, up close?"

"We have no choice but to find out," the captain said. "We seem to have inherited the *Enterprise*'s mission, whether we like it or not. We've got this ship, and we've got unexplored light minutes through which to creep, and we've got a faith to keep."

"A faith? With whom? With the Federation?"

"Yes, and with ourselves—and with . . ." She swept her gaze up the sky, again—up the river in the sky—again. She turned her back on her lieutenant and slid uphill, toward the bridge.

"With whom?" Jee called after her. "With whom?" she insisted.

"Let's go somewhere," Captain Dalen replied to her shipmate. "Thataway."

Afterword

by George Zebrowski

A Dyson Sphere, for those of you who may be unfamiliar with all the large imaginary artifacts to be found in science fiction, is the rest of a Ringworld, which is only a ribbon cut out from the equator of a sphere. Named after Freeman Dyson, one of the great scientists and writers of this century, the sphere fulfills the definition of a Type II Civilization—one that effectively uses all the energy of its star. Type I uses the power of its planet; Type III, the power of a galaxy. We are not even Type I.

Larry Niven's Ringworld (from the 1970 novel of the same name) is an ingenious in-between Type I and Type II civilization artifact—an equatorial strip cut out of a Dyson Sphere, perhaps part of a sphere that was never completed, after the builders saw how much it would take to finish the job! The Ringworld also provides an incredible amount of land area; but it pales in comparison with a Dyson Sphere.

A profound question comes up for the novelist who tries to make use of a Dyson Sphere for dramatic purposes: What is there of interest to do with a Dyson Sphere? And this inevitably includes the bigger question: What would a culture want to do with a Dyson Sphere? Why would it wish to build one?

The history of science fiction is filled with large structures; but it is a mistake to consider them as mere genre conceits, "big dumb objects," as some have called them, growing out of the desire to have purely fictional dramatic extravagances to put before jaded readers.

On the contrary, all the large structures of science fiction emerge from seriously meant speculations questioning the future of human habitats, with our given planet being only one such (not of our making), but which we insist on altering (primarily through the growth of cities).

The central questions that we are answering, both in our imaginings and in the way we have used the Earth, are "Where is there to live?" and "How shall we arrange our living space?" And even, "Where and how does intelligent life choose to live in this universe?" The ultimate end of such questions is, "What shall we live for? What does any intelligent life live for?"

The poet's ultimate answer is to dream of pulling down the world entire and remaking it closer to our heart's desire. But the universe has a few laws that do not reconcile with the poet's wishes. We have, however, shown a remarkable ability of accomplishing what in past ages would have been considered miracles. No monarch of centuries past traveled as much as many of us do, or listened to as much music, or saw so much with the magic lanterns of our movie and television screens, or even merely looked at as many beautiful men and women as the most ordinary of us see in films and magazines in the course of a month. Medical miracles are routine. There is no need to prove that we are tending to remake ourselves as well as our world, and that we will continue to do so, even to the point of attempting to circumvent or perhaps change physical laws in some far distant future. It's a rob Peter to pay Paul entropic universe, but we don't like that and sometimes behave as if it were not true. Our human minds and cultures run against entropy toward greater organization, seeking permanence and knowledge against the darkness.

So we do not doubt that a Dyson Sphere or a Ringworld might be attempted by some intelligent species in the universe. Altering themselves and the physical reality around it may be the habitual behavior of all intelligent life in the universe!

The essay by my co-author that follows my words here suggests, among other things, how one might answer my earlier question, "What can a science fiction writer do with a Dyson Sphere in a work of fiction?" The answer is that one must think about the physical possibilities of a Dyson Sphere habitat, to the point where one can see the implications for life on the inner surface, as we might see by studying the desert Bedouin and understanding how that environment shaped their lives and cultures. It is only then that the most provocative and enlightening dramatic possibilities may be plucked from the data, however imaginary but possible the assumptions.

This is one reason I have chosen to work with Charles Pellegrino in recent years. His work in various sciences, when combined with human implications, yields new and authentic stories of humankind's possible liberation from its historical mires. Realistic, convincing SF does enable us to see through time; not perfectly, but in ways that avoid the gratuitous, self-referencing forms of SF that cannot see beyond themselves, and which, being cut off from the cutting edge of critical knowledge, contribute to the growth of ignorance and superstition and the increase of clouded minds.

Have we taken liberties with the known in this novel?

Yes, we have.

Why have we done so?

To mark the places of our human ignorance that will be filled in by futurity, because ignorance is itself a map of possibilities. We need that map, to keep us both honest, and yet open to what is possible. But in serious SF we must mark the territory of our ignorance carefully, and surround that territory with what we in fact do know. In mathematics, equations with multiple unknowns are solvable because they have been shaped to flush out the answer. Another way of saying that ignorance is itself a map is to say that we must ask the right questions, ones that look outward to the universe according to our best knowledge, wherever it may lead, while keeping in mind our own inner failings. The critical method of "err and correct" that is modern science is the best reality check we have, and yet almost everywhere in human affairs it is both subverted and ignored.

The battle is still in progress, and one sign of hope is that there is a struggle going on.

George Zebrowski
Albany, New York
August 8, 1998

Afterword

Reality Check

by Charles Pellegrino

The human race is a remarkable creature, one with great potential, and I hope that Star Trek *has helped to show us what we can be if we believe in ourselves and our abilities.*

—GENE RODDENBERRY

About the same time Gene Roddenberry was coming up with his idea for "a *Wagon Train* in space series," I was learning an important lesson in nuclear physics—or the thermonuclear inverse to the Golden Rule—call it what you will; and let me tell you something: I was scared to death.

I was eight years old, then, and the Cuban Missile Crisis was in full bloom. At P.S. 23, in Flushing, the teachers had given us dog tags, and one of those diabolical "bomb wardens" seemed to delight in telling us that the tags could withstand very high temperatures, meaning that we would be identifiable among the dead if we misbehaved, and failed to *duck and cover* in time, and became carbonized shadows on the school walls.

My best friend at that time was a Cuban refugee named Carlos—who had seen half his family killed personally by Fidel Castro. And as we practiced our duck and cover skills in the halls of P.S. 23, a life-size bronze statue of none other than Fidel Castro stood watch over us, stood beside the American flag, near the principal's office. It stood there because two of Castro's nephews were attending the high school across the street. (Or something like that. Something strange.)

"Castro is coming," my friend said. "He has big guns. *Big guns and big bombs.*"

What I will never forget, what I will take with me as long as I live, is how high and squeaky his voice became as he said it. I was only eight years old. And I was scared to death. And yet I laughed.

"Who is laughing over there?" shouted the teacher with the unhealthy interest in dog tag vaporization points.

I filed this away for future reference—RULE: *There must be no laughing during a nuclear holocaust.* And I began to believe that one probably had to go really, really nuts in order to become a grownup.

Into that nutty world (thank whatever gods may be) came Gene Roddenberry with his off-beat t.v. series. I remember having bad dreams (and worse daydreams) about a day in the not too distant future when my grandmother's granite tombstone would glow ghostly red under the firestorm, and I envied her for having grown old and died before she could become witness to the death of her entire civilization. I suspected that if any of my generation survived, our children would inherit a radioactive wilderness. And then came this visionary—this Roddenberry—showing us an alternate future in which Russians and Americans and other "modern day antagonists" would live and work together in space, a future in which it was possible to believe that our civilization, if it was wise and paid attention, might not merely survive, but might actually excel.

Years later, Jim Powell, Hiroshi Takahashi (both of Brookhaven National Laboratory), Pierre Noyes (of the Stanford Linear Accelerator), and I had designed the world's first practical antimatter rocket. Rather than flee the world of sub-atomic particles and high-energy physics, I ultimately embraced it. I think the hopeful future Gene Roddenberry pointed to had more than a little bit to do with putting me on that path: and in homage to him, I gave some of the ship's components names that were already familiar to viewers of *Star Trek*. Hence, the antihydrogen containment units became "antimatter pods."

The Valkyrie, as our rocket is called, will have a maximum cruising speed of 92 percent lightspeed—which is a nice speed at which to be traveling because the crew (a maximum of four to each spacecraft, though most likely two) will be aging at only one-third the rate of stay-at-home observers on Earth. While this can mean six years of back taxes for every two years of flight pay, it also means that the nearer stars will be reachable in travel times comparable to those already experienced by Charles Darwin aboard the *Beagle,* and by Charles Wayville aboard the H.M.S. *Challenger.*

At this time, we have seen no hints of a universe that will allow anything so large as a molecule of water to achieve lightspeed (the real-life equivalent of warp speed, at which light itself becomes ageless), and to survive the journey. But the fact remains that relativistic rockets—actual starships—can be built without having to climb over the hurdle of inventing a new physics. The Valkyries should be flying by the year 2050. If our civilization really is wise, and really does pay attention, then something very much like the voyages of discovery envisioned by Gene Roddenberry will begin in our lifetimes. We can build a future that anyone living today would be proud of. Human beings are perfectible, and I do believe we are moving (albeit slowly, albeit painfully) in that direction.

It has therefore been a great honor to co-author a *Star Trek* novel with George Zebrowski, a man who trips over more fascinating, forward-looking ideas when he climbs out of bed each morning than most people have over the course of an entire decade. To say nothing of the fact that, having co-designed an actual starship (a sure sign that I've watched too many episodes of *Star Trek*), I simply had to write this story. *Had* to. Call it a thank you letter to Gene.

Now, about that starship. Let me show you how it is done, and why it should be done, and why the near future may be even more fantastical than most science fiction writers have imagined.

Until very recently, most scientists simply dismissed the notion that crewed spacecraft would ever be able to cover interstellar distances and return in a reasonable amount of time. To most people (even to scientists) the distance across the Atlantic Ocean, from New York to London, seems large. That's nearly 6560 kilometers, but it can be traversed by a beam of light in just under one forty-sixth of a second. The ocean, for all its frightful majesty, reaches barely one-sixth of the way around the Earth's almost 41,000 kilometer circumference. The distance from the Atlantic Ocean to the Sea of Tranquillity on the moon is nearly ten times the circumference of the Earth, about 410,000 kilometers, or one-and-a-half seconds away at the speed of light. Mars, on its closest approach to Earth, is almost five light minutes away, or two hundred times the distance to the moon. The distance to the nearest star system, the Alpha Centauri trinary, is 41 trillion kilometers—about four-and-a-half light years, or a half million times the distance to Mars. And that is the *nearest* star system.

As I write, a new generation of telescopes is revealing what the creator of *Star Trek* seemed to have known all along: Earth is not unique, for almost every star in the sky appears to be orbited by planets. Even if almost all of those planets are as lifeless as the sands of the moon and Mercury, then across the span of a galaxy 25,000 times as wide as the distance separating Earth from Alpha Centauri, the existence of other Earthlike worlds is, given enough throws of the cosmic dice, statistically inevitable; and beyond our galaxy, at a distance only twenty times the diameter of the Milky Way, lies the Andromeda Galaxy—*another* island of 600 million stars—and beyond Andromeda, for more than eight billion light years, upward of 300 billion galaxies fill the visible universe. And that is the *visible* universe.

Take this, therefore, as a mathematical certainty: we are not alone.

And strangest of all to think that we may soon be able to go out there—to "go thataway," and to finally answer the question, "Who goes there?"

Failing the discovery of something akin to "subspace" we will be forced to obey, in our exploration, the seemingly unbreakable laws of relativity—which gives us a universe limited by the speed of light.

This is not a reason for despair. The Dooglasse ship, as depicted in this novel, managed quite well, and if one looks closely enough, one sees that it is in fact an antimatter propelled Valkyrie (most relativistic rockets, just like most supersonic transport jets, are bound to look alike).

Most of the equipment for the rocket itself can be assembled using today's technology. Providing the fuel, however, becomes problematic. We would require an array of solar powered linear accelerators ("atom smashers") girdling the moon's equator. Mega-engineering projects require, in their own turn, miniature self-replicating factories that draw building materials directly from the lunar soil. Current advances in robot technology teach us that we should be able to climb this technological hurdle by about 2025. The brains of ants and wasps, working far more efficiently than today's chess champion computers, are already capable of performing all of the essential analyses and motions that make possible the production of self-replicating machines. Within those microscopic bundles of insect nerves lie the keys to a technological advance that will make very large lunar arrays (named Asimov Arrays, after the scientist/author who corrected a major mathematical error the week we invented them) as feasible and inexpensive as the cost of developing the first thirty machines—which can then be sent to the construction site, somewhat like a viral infection.

(We can probably do this, and we probably should, but . . .)

Pierre Noyes, who worked with Freeman Dyson on Project Orion (an interplanetary ancestor of Valkyrie that utilized fission bombs), cautions that once humanity instills an antlike intelligence into its machines, mutations among their replicants—and an evolutionary process far more rapid than anything the Earth has seen in biological organisms—may commence. "We may be unable to prevent it," he says. "Try to imagine a million years of evolution taking place in very smart ants overnight."

Why is it that science fiction doesn't seem quite so strange anymore?

What makes it possible for the realities of scientific achievement (Valkyrie rockets) to catch up with the fiction (starships) is that Valkyrie is the ultralight of rockets, consisting mostly of naked magnetic coils and pods held together by tethers. Indeed, it can best be summed up as a kite (with magnetic field lines instead of paper sheets) that flies through space on a muon wind of its own creation. Earlier starship designs by space scientists Donald Goldsmith, Tobias Owen, and others yielded estimates that a journey to the nearest star would require 400 million tons of matter-antimatter fuel and would be barely capable of reaching ten percent lightspeed, leading to flight times of several decades. Such estimates arose from traditional rocket configurations (huge, reinforced towers, with engines welded to their feet), which resulted in prohibitively heavy, slow-moving vehicles. Thus did more that 99.7 percent of their mass become fuel. Our stripped down Valkyrie's fuel stores (both matter and anti-matter combined) are estimated at slightly less than half the mass of the rest of the spacecraft, or about one hundred tons.

The engine is simply a magnetic coil, which generates a magnetic field, against which particles from the matter-antimatter reaction zone are bounced. The magnetic field (and hence the coil), is propelled forward by the bounce. The coil then pulls the rest of the ship along on a string, much as a motorboat pulls a water skier. A pulling rather than a pushing engine eliminates most of the structural girders that would not only, by their mere existence, add unwarranted mass, but would multiply that mass many times over by their need for shields and cooling equipment, and by added fuel to push the added equipment, and by added fuel to push the added fuel . . . leading to a chain reaction of design complications . . . and to an engine that burns hotter, but which cannot afford to push the giant to even a significant fraction of lightspeed. By contrast to what has traditionally become known as the large, slow-moving "space ark" approach to interstellar flight, Valkyrie becomes a low mass speedboat.

The primary propellant for Valkyrie, the antiproton, is not merely a figment of the science fiction writer's imagination; though, as is often the case, science fiction writers seem to have discovered it long ahead of the scientists (Gene Roddenberry is the first person, to my knowledge, to have anticipated antimatter's practicality in spacecraft propulsion).

At this time, small numbers of antiprotons are routinely produced in physics experiments. In atomic accelerators, they are magnetically confined (or bottled), cooled, and stabilized by combination with antielectrons (called positrons; see Data's brain), to produce antihydrogen atoms.

An antihydrogen atom is the antimatter twin of the more familiar hydrogen atom, but its electron (positron) is positively charged and its negatively charged proton (an antiproton) also has a charge opposite that of a normal hydrogen nucleus. Since matter and antimatter annihilate each other on contact, each converting 100 percent of its mass into energy and near-lightspeed particles (at which point even a tiny chip of proton can deliver a force equivalent to being struck by a New York City taxicab), and since each, on contact, releases enormous bursts of energy from literally microscopic amounts of propellant, one cannot simply fill a space shuttle's tanks with several tons of liquid antihydrogen and let it slosh around inside (Note: this would be bad).

The only storage method that has a hope of working is solid antihydrogen, supercooled within one degree of absolute zero (within one Kelvin of -273 degrees C). At very low temperatures, antihydrogen condenses into "white flake," with an extremely low vaporization rate.

Particles of solid antihydrogen can be suspended and held away from the "pod" walls by electrostatic forces and/or magnetism. Within 0.0005 degrees K., antihydrogen appears sufficiently stable to allow storage and mixture, as microscopic fuel wafers, with actual matter, and although this matter of storage was once considered as the basis for a potential engine design, visions of outward bound starships blossoming into red-shifting novae raised too many hairs on the backs of our necks and led us to decide: "Don't go there." This, despite the fact that in 1984 we were discovering, to our surprise, that matter-antimatter reactants quickly flew apart, once the reaction began, making the reaction itself seemingly impossible to sustain.

An almost identical problem faced colleagues trying to sustain controlled fusion: it worked only if one wanted to create a short, powerful burst. The universe seems to delight in handing civilization such cruel jokes. Turning a new energy source into a bomb is easy, a no-brainer. If you want to build an engine, or an accident-proof reactor, you have to think a lot harder. Our problem led to a very complex Valkyrie Mark II engine design, in which micro-wafers had to be assembled from matter and antimatter immediately prior to use, then fired—up to sixty wafers per second—into a laser-warmed reaction zone. This led to a new problem, almost identical to one encountered by World War One aircraft engineers trying to figure out how best to fire bullets through the propeller of a plane without shooting off the propeller (except that antimatter multiplied this problem a hundred fold). As the engine grew more complex, so too did its safety systems, so too did its mass, meaning more fuel and more firings per second, meaning more complexity, and so on, and so on. Our physics was clearly leading us in the wrong direction.

By 1993, the Brookhaven National Laboratory Valkyrie sessions had led me and Jim Powell to a few items we had never intended to invent (two of which are hinted at in this novel). Along the way, we were nicknamed "the Salvador Dali and Pablo Picasso of nukes." Then, in 1994, "Rembrandt" asked if he could join us. Powell and I, when we worked together during a Valkyrie jam session, seemed to communicate in the kind of shortspeak often said to occur between identical twins. The result was not Jim plus Charles (one plus one) equals two—but, rather, "Jim and Charles squared." When Pierre Noyes joined the sessions, something even more magical occurred: We were cubed.

Cutting one another off in mid-sentence and completing our sentences for one another, we managed to simplify the Valkyrie's antimatter core by a factor of a hundred, in a single afternoon. Along the way, Pierre began to wonder what would happen if we aimed the world's most powerful laser directly into the path of gamma rays shooting out of a proton-antiproton reaction zone. When he went back to Stanford, the collision was arranged: photons of light (massless units which, while traveling at lightspeed, manifest simultaneously—and self-contradictorily—as both particles and waves) collided with photons of light, their power sufficient to spin photons off as electrons and positrons. The world's first absorbic reaction, the conversion of energy to matter, is no longer science fiction (oh, goody—another brave new bomb, if we are unwise, and fail to pay attention).

One result of "Dali, Picasso, and Rembrandt cubed" has been the Valkyrie Mark III engine—about which we are finally able to release some details. And what better people to tell first, than the *Star Trek* audience?

Mark III is quite simple, actually. Temperature regulation in the antimatter pods will control how fast or slow antihydrogen white flake is permitted to evaporate. As the evaporated antihydrogen leaves the magnetic bottle, and is guided toward the magnetic gun barrel of an atomic accelerator, the atoms are ionized and stripped of their positrons. The positrons are simply ejected into space (for, if allowed to react with electrons, they will produce powerful gamma rays while providing essentially zero thrust). The antiprotons are accelerated to approximately 750 kilometers per second, and when they arrive at the reaction zone, behave somewhat like slow relativistic bombs (mark this as an oxymoron, albeit an essential one). At this velocity, the antiprotons pass like ghosts through beryllium windows, hardly noticing that they have passed through anything at all. They detonate when they reach ("and stick to") the hydrogen nuclei behind the windows; and by carefully controlling the number of antiprotons reaching the hydrogen (by regulating evaporation rates in the antimatter pods), and hence controlling the temperature of the hydrogen target, the result becomes a finely tuned fusion reaction— in effect, an antimatter-triggered hydrogen bomb that, instead of exploding, merely glows, at any rate one wants it to glow.

That glow is in fact a spray of (for our purposes) reasonably massive charged particles, among them helium nuclei. Just as the antiprotons shooting in through the beryllium window fail to notice that a container wall exists, any fusion products shooting out (at the still relatively slow velocity of 12 to 20 percent lightspeed), depart like beams of light exiting glass. The particles then bounce off the ship's forward magnetic field, giving away their energy as thrust.

As the ship's speedometer begins to climb above twelve to twenty percent the velocity of light, fusion ions, though more massive than the products of straightforward proton-antiproton annihilation, decline significantly in propulsion efficiency. To push the Valkyrie to a higher fraction of lightspeed, higher exhaust velocities are needed. At this point, the Mark III reaction mix depends less and less upon fusion, until ultimately it shifts purely to proton-antiproton pairing. At this point, the less efficient reaction (which sheds low mass particles at high speed), has become the more efficient reaction, if for no other reason than it is our only choice.

The reaction products, traveling at high relativistic speed (the speed we want to get our rocket up to) consist of elementary particles called mesons. Each meson has a mass intermediate between a proton and an electron. It is essentially a proton fragment gone so relativistic (read, ballistic) that it is at once a particle and a wave, and some of its quarks and gluons have dispersed into the universe as energy (read, massless photons and neutrinos). The matter-antimatter spray produces three varieties, or "flavors," of pi-mesons.

1. Neutral pi-mesons comprise thirty percent of the proton-antiproton reaction products. They decay immediately into gamma rays.
2. Positively charged pi-mesons, traveling near the speed of light, decay into positively charged mu-mesons (muons) and neutrinos after flying, on average, only twenty-one meters. The muons last several microseconds (almost two kilometers) before decaying into positively charged electrons and neutrinos.
3. Negatively charged pi-mesons behave the same way positively charged ones do, except that the resulting muons and electrons are negatively charged.

The charged *pions* and *muons* are the particles we want, and preferably we want the innermost fringes of the engine's magnetic field (or magnetic pusher plate) to reach within twenty-one meters of the reaction zone, so that it can steal whatever thrust the pions have to contribute before a significant fraction of them have decayed and shed some of their energy as useless neutrinos.

One reason for our ship being built from a tether system is that the engine sheds lethal doses of gamma rays. Riding an antimatter rocket is like riding a giant death ray bomb: you want to put as much distance as possible between yourself and the engine. Suspending the crew compartment, antimatter pods, and other major, radiation-sensitive elements on the end of a ten kilometer-long tether allows the engine to dissipate most of its rays directly into space, and shaves off many tons of shielding. Further protection is gained by strapping a tiny block of (let us say) tungsten to the tether, about one hundred meters behind the matter-antimatter reaction zone. Gamma rays are attenuated by a factor of ten for every two centimeters of tungsten they pass through. Therefore, a block of tungsten twenty centimeters deep will reduce the gamma dose to anything behind it by a factor of ten to the tenth power. An important shielding advantage provided by a ten kilometer-long tether is that, by locating the tungsten shield one hundred times closer to the engine than the crew, the diameter of the shield need only be one-hundredth the diameter of the gamma ray shadow (or eclipse) we want to cast over and around the crew compartment. *The weight of the shielding system then becomes trivial.*

Gamma rays will, however, knock atoms out of position in structures near the engine, making coils, tethers, and maintenance equipment stronger, yet brittle. This will probably require additional tungsten plugs and rings (called shadow shields, these gamma ray eclipsers are already being used in certain very advanced nuclear reactors). Another supplemental solution is to weave most structures residing within four kilometers of the engine from hundreds of filaments, and to send electric currents through the filaments, heating them, one at a time, to several hundredths of a degree below their melting point. Gamma ray displacements in the wires are thus rearranged, and the atoms can reestablish their normal positions.

There appears to be nothing we can do, however, to prevent the occasional transmutations of atoms into other elements. Fly far enough with your engines burning at full throttle, and your ship will slowly turn into gold, plus lithium, arsenic, chlorine, and a lot of other elements that were not aboard when you left. These new substances will be concentrated around the antimatter reaction zone, and it is important to note that advanced composite materials already coming into existence dictate that Valkyrie, even at this early design stage, will be built mostly from ceramic and organic composite materials, rather than from metals.

It is likely that expanding knowledge of composites will be taken into account by the time relativistic spacecraft are actually being built, so that the ships will incorporate any transmuted elements into their filaments in a manner that ultimately results in structural improvements for vessels designed (by aid of sophisticated tether relays and robot technology) to essentially rebuild themselves as they fly. Exploiting what seems at first glance to be a disadvantage (transmutation) is simply a matter of anticipating the "disadvantage" before you begin to build. It's the disadvantages unforeseen (the questions unasked) that threaten to jump up and pull you down.

Valkyrie's tether system requires that elements of the ship be designed to climb "up" and "down" the lines, somewhat like elevators on tracks. There is an irony involved in this configuration. Our "inside-out" rocket—with its engine ahead of the fuel tanks and its fuel tanks ahead of its payload—is nothing new. We have simply come full circle and rediscovered Robert Goddard's original rocket configuration. Nor is the engine's magnetic field nozzle an entirely new creation. It guides and focuses jets of subatomic particles in the same way that the tool of choice among microbiologists guides streams of electrons through magnetic lenses. Valkyrie, in essence, is little more than a glorified electron microscope.

* * *

Flying through space at a significant fraction of lightspeed is like looking down the barrel of a super particle collider. Even an isolated proton has a sting, and grains of sand begin to resemble torpedoes. Judging from what is presently known about interstellar space, such torpedoes will certainly be encountered, perhaps as frequently as once a day. Valkyrie does not have the *Enterprise*'s force shields, nor can we dumb energy harmlessly into "subspace." Add to the interstellar dust problem, the fact that as energy from the engine (particularly gamma radiation) shines into the shadow shields and other ship components, the heat it deposits must be ejected.

Jim Powell and I have a system that can perform both services (particle shielding and heat shedding), at least during the acceleration and cruise phases of flight. We can dump intercepted engine heat into a fluid (chiefly organic material with metallic inclusions) and throw streams of hot droplets out ahead of the ship. The droplets radiate their heat load into space before the ship accelerates into and recaptures them in magnetic funnels for eventual re-use. These same, heat-shedding droplets will ionize most of the atoms they encounter by stripping off their electrons. The rocket itself then shunts the resulting shower of particles—protons and electrons—off to either side of its magnetic field, in much the same manner as a boat's prow pushes aside water.

When an interstellar dust grain impacts against

the droplet field, far ahead of the ship, the particles from which the grain is made simply behave as individual particles, "unaware" that they are part of anything else. Hence, as dust penetrates the droplet, each proton, electron and neutron will scatter, their angle of scatter increasing as the particles pass through more and more droplets in their approach to Valkyrie's magnetic field. We need only worry about neutrons or other unchanged particles that plunge through the magnetic field lines and impact the coil and other engine parts on the nose of the ship, where they will deposit heat—which we expel on a spray of reusable droplets.

One of the great advantages of a droplet shield is that it is consistently renewing itself. Put a dent in it, and the cavity is immediately filled by the outrushing spray.

Valkyrie is designed to carry a spare engine, located at the aft end of its ten kilometer-long tether. The forward engine pulls the ship along during the acceleration phase of flight. It also fires during the cruise phase, but only at one thousandth of a gravity, keeping the tether taut and permitting recapture of the forward-flying droplets. At the end of the cruise phase of flight, the crew compartment, antimatter pods and shadow shields are rearranged along the tether, and the aft engine begins its (months-long) deceleration burn. The spare provides a rescue capability, and eliminates the difficulty of swinging a ten kilometer-long ship broadside to relativistic bombardment, in order to turn the engine around and fire in reverse.

At this stage, empty fuel pods, weighing several tons and no longer in use, will consume fuel if they are decelerated with the rest of the ship. Since new pods and return propellant (at least the matter component—which is in fact the lion's share of the ship's fuel reserve) can be manufactured and replaced at the destination solar system, the pods will be ground up into ultrafine dust and dumped overboard. At up to ninety-two percent the speed of light, the dust will fly ahead of the decelerating ship, exploding interstellar grains and clearing a temporary path (trajectory must be such that relativistic dust streams will dissipate and fly out of the galaxy without passing near stars and risking detonation in the atmospheres of planets).

This fist of relativistic dust is the first line of defense against particles encountered during final approach. With the aft engine firing into the direction of flight, fields of droplet spray will become useful only for expelling heat from the aft engine, for along the tether, "up" has now become "down," and the droplets can only be sprayed "up," behind the engine, where, traveling at uniform speed, they will fall back upon the decelerating ship. To shield against particles and grains ahead of the ship, ultrathin "umbrellas," made of organic polymers similar to mylar and stacked thousands of layers deep, must be lowered into the direction of flight.

This is the second line of defense—against particles drifting into the ever-lengthening column of space between the ship and the "fist." The umbrellas will behave much like the droplet shield and, in like manner, they will be designed with rapid self-repair in mind.

During the cruise phase of flight, pseudogravity is produced by rotating the entire crew compartment (which is also the landing vehicle, with living accommodations approximately equal to a one bedroom apartment) on a harness (counterbalanced with supplies) to produce a force equivalent to one Earth gravity (or one g). The two crew members (presumably husband and wife) will probably have to weigh in at or below 55 kilograms, in order to best endure the two g acceleration required to reach the 92 percent cruising speed, and then to decelerate down from it. Both the acceleration and deceleration phases of flight last for six months, as experienced by outside observers (slightly less for the crew: at 70 percent lightspeed, the crew are already aging nearly one third slower than the rest of the universe; at 92 percent c, they age only one day for every three days experienced on Earth).

This may sound grueling to some, but there are many people (myself included) who would be willing to make such journeys, to worlds we would already know (given the current rate of advance in long-range planetary observation) to be worth exploring. And, given an on-board storage capacity for the accumulated art, music, history, film, and literature of our entire civilization, we will be traveling with luxuries Charles Darwin and the librarians of Alexandria would have envied.

And there you have it. In our lifetime: interstellar flight, *Star Trek*—call it what you will; and we shall have it, too, if only we are wise, and pay attention.

There will be differences between the reality and the fiction, to be sure. Slower travel times? Almost certainly. Transporters? Not likely. But we may find that we are not troubled by Einstein and Hawking's travel restrictions. Sometimes reality has a way of sneaking up on us and surpassing fiction. Gene Roddenberry imagined futuristic medical facilities that begin to look more familiar each passing year, yet he did not foresee how soon we would (Khan aside) reach the genetic frontier, where we have begun, now, to find hints that the aging process can be slowed significantly, perhaps stopped, perhaps even reversed. Jim Powell, my partner on Valkyrie (and the man who first suggested turning my "clones-from-amber recipe" into a dinosaur theme park), believes that there is no theoretical limit to how long humans can live. Even sooner, we may be able to artificially boost human intelligence. Power and peril. Promise and responsibility. This is the world we are coming to, and it is not for the timid.

I know of a place where the lava is water, and where lakes are gasoline. It orbits Saturn with tides that put the Bay of Fundy to shame. In a few years, we shall drop a flock of robot helicopters into its atmosphere.

I know of volcanically-warmed oceans, hidden beneath the ice of Enceladus and Europa, and we should not be shocked, when our robot submarines finally penetrate the ice, if we find crablike and fishlike creatures there.

I know of a bacterial consortium, interconnected by a circulatory system more than a city block long, that has begun, at a furious rate, to mine sulfur and iron from the *Titanic*'s hull plates, turning the ship's minerals into the substance of biology, and turning the ship itself into one of the largest organisms on Earth (second only to the fungus that underlies a good part of Michigan). Through this strangest of all living fossils, we can look back across four billion years and see that the phenomenon we call multicellular life appears to have been pulled from a disarmingly simple bag of tricks, and we can look outward and outward from our Earth and see that the universe must be teeming with creatures that breathe and swim and talk.

I know that electrons coursing through our neural grids make it possible to read these words. They are the basis of every thought we have, somehow producing a mind that, as it asks questions about the universe and designs computers to help answer them, feels quite separate from the nerve cells and electrons themselves. The electrons are working in our best interests, supposedly; but perhaps it is they, and not you, not me, who are really thinking about these words.

Maybe our bodies are little more than vessels serving their interests, and as we set forth to design increasingly advanced artificial brains (ancestors to Data, perhaps), it becomes possible to believe that the *sine qua non* of our existence is to build faster, less bulky, more mobile electron vessels, perhaps even to eventually clear the decks for them, as the dinosaurs once cleared the decks for us.

I know of particles that appear to tunnel backward, over very short distances, through time; and beyond them I (or "merely" the electrons in my head, trying to understand where they came from) have peered with Stephen Hawking, Arthur C. Clarke and the Jesuit Mervin Fernando into the basement of the universe—peered beyond quarks, beyond gluons, to an absolute limit of smallness, at one million billion billionth of an inch. "Physics," the Jesuit said—"It is our destiny to know the universe." But . . . "I don't think that physics tells us how to behave to our neighbors," the physicist replied. "Ah," quipped Arthur Clarke, "but physics may determine who our neighbors are and on what planets they live!"

I know of apparent paradoxes in the age and structure of the universe (hopefully more apparent than real) that have revived the idea of multiple quantum dimensions, and brought to life hypotheses about "quantum subspace" and a "pretzel universe," in which light from a given object has so many different paths through which to reach us that it can propagate as multiple copies. If these paradoxes turn out not to be mere mathematical aberrations, then the universe may be smaller and stranger than we have been led to believe and, in principle, we could look out to the very edge of space and see our own solar system.

There are wonders, out there, of which you and I have scarcely begun to dream; and some of them are closer than you think.

Charles Pellegrino
New York, New York
July 20, 1998

Selected Bibliography

Asimov, I., C. Pellegrino, J. Powell, *et al.* May 1986 American Association for the Advancement of Science Symposium on *Interstellar Travel and Communication.* (Includes reports by John Rather, Jill Tarter [on whom Carl Sagan based his lead character in *Contact*], Robert Jastrow and Robert Forward; reprints, tapes available through AAAS.)

Clarke, A.C., S. Hawking, Fr. M. Fernando, "God, the Universe, and Everything" in *Return to Sodom and Gomorrah,* C. Pellegrino, Avon Books, New York, 1994.

Cosmovici, C., S. Bowyer and D. Werthimer eds., *Astronomical and Biochemical Origins and the Search for Life in the Universe: Proceedings of the 5th International Conference on Bioastronomy (IAU Colloquium 161).* Editrice Compositori, 1997.

Hawking, S., "The Beginning of the Universe," in Texas/ESO-CERN Symposium on Relativistic Astrophysics, Cosmology, and Fundamental Physics. New York: *Annals of the New York Academy of Sciences* [647], 1991.

Margulis, L. *Ghia in Oxford II: The Evolution of the Superorganism,* Oxford, 1997.

Marinatos, S. *Some Words about the Legend of Atlantis.* Athens: Athens Museum, 1969.

Pellegrino, C.R. and J. Powell, "Making Star Trek Real," *Analog,* September, 1986.

Pellegrino, C. and R. Cullimore, "The Rebirth of R.M.S. Titanic: A Study of the Bioarchaeology of a Physically Disrupted Sunken Vessel," *Voyage,* June 1997. (Details contained in this report are not only relevant to this novel, but these are annals from the voyages of the oceanographic Research Vessel *Voyager*—and yes, we really did have a French cook named Neelix.)

Silleck, B. and J. Marvin, *Cosmic Voyage* (VIDEO; IMAX/Smithsonian: To date, the finest film available depicting time and space and our place in it).

Wooley, L., *Dead Cities and Living Men,* New York, William Morrow and Company, 1956.

About the Authors

Charles Pellegrino wears many hats. He has been known to work simultaneously in crustaceology, paleontology, preliminary design of advanced rocket systems, and marine archaeology. He has been described by Stephen Jay Gould as a space scientist who occasionally looks down and by Arthur C. Clarke as "the polymathic astro-geologist-nuclear physicist who happens to be the world's first astro-paleontologist." He was, with James Powell, Harvey Meyerson, and the late Senator Spark Matsunaga, a framer of the U.S.-Russian Space Cooperation Initiative (which included, among its designs, an International Space Station and joint Mars missions). At Brookhaven National Laboratory he and Dr. James Powell coordinate brainstorming sesssions on the next seventy years; projects currently under design by Powell and Pellegrino range from a global system of high-speed Maglev trains (New York to Sydney in five hours) to relativistic flight (Valkyrie rockets) and the raising of an archaeological site (the wreckage of a Portuguese galleon and the mud that contained it) completely intact from a quarter mile under the Atlantic Ocean.

In the late 1970s Dr. Pellegrino and Dr. Jesse A. Stoff produced the original models that predicted the discovery of oceans inside certain moons of Jupiter and Saturn. While looking at the requirements for robot exploration of those new oceans, Pellegrino sailed with Dr. Robert Ballard, worked with the deep-sea robot *Argo,* and traced the *Titanic* debris field backward in time to reconstruct the liner's last three minutes. He has since, with James Powell, developed an economically viable means of raising and displaying the *Titanic*'s four-hundred-foot-long bow section.

Through his work on ancient DNA (including a recipe involving dinosaur cells that may be preserved in mouth parts and in the stomachs of ninety-five-million-year-old amberized flies), Pellegrino hopes one day to redefine extinction. His hope—and his recipe—became the basis for the Michael Crichton novel/Stephen Spielberg film *Jurassic Park.*

Among his nonfiction books are *Unearthing Atlantis, Time Gate, Return to Sodom and Gomorrah,* and the *New York Times* bestseller *Her Name, Titanic,* which became a basis for James Cameron's motion picture *Titanic.* His novels include *Flying to Valhalla, Dust,* and, with George Zebrowski, *The Killing Star.* He is currently working on projects with James Cameron.

George Zebrowski's thirty books include novels, short fiction collections, anthologies, and a book of essays. Science fiction writer Greg Bear calls him "one of those rare speculators who bases his dreams on science as well as inspiration," and the late Terry Carr, one of the most influential science fiction editors of recent years, described him as "an authority in the SF field." Zebrowski has published more than sixty works of short fiction and more than a hundred articles and essays. His work has appeared in every major science fiction magazine, and most notably in the *Bertrand Russell Society News.*

His best known novel is *Macrolife,* which Arthur C. Clarke described as "a worthy successor to Olaf Stapledon's *Star Maker.* It's been years since I was so impressed. One of the few books I intend to read again." *Library Journal* chose *Macrolife* as one of the one hundred best science fiction novels, and The Easton Press reissued it in its "Masterpieces of Science Fiction" series. Zebrowski's stories and novels have been translated into a half-dozen languages; his short fiction has been nominated for the Nebula Award and the Theodore Sturgeon Memorial Award. *Stranger Suns* was a *New York Times* Notable Book of the Year.

The Killing Star, written with scientist/author Charles Pellegrino, received unanimous praise in national newspapers and magazines. *The New York Times Book Review,* which included *The Killing Star* on its Recommended Summer Reading list, called it "a novel of such conceptual ferocity and scientific plausibility that it amounts to a reinvention of that old Wellsian staple, [alien invasion] . . ." *The Washington Post Book World* described the novel as "a classic SF theme pushed logically to its ultimate conclusions."

The Borgo Press brought out *The Work of George Zebrowski: An Annotated Bibliography and Guide* (Third Edition) and *Beneath the Red Star,* his collection of essays on international SF, in conjunction with his appearance as Guest of Honor at the Science Fiction Research Association Conference.

His new novel is *Brute Orbits* (HarperPrism). Forthcoming in 1999 are *Skylife: Visions of Our Homes in Space,* edited with Gregory Benford (Harcourt Brace). The long awaited companion novel to *Macrolife, Cave of Stars,* will also be published by HarperPrism.

Look for STAR TREK Fiction from Pocket Books

Star Trek®: The Original Series

Star Trek: The Next Generation®

Encounter at Farpoint • David Gerrold
Unification • Jeri Taylor
Relics • Michael Jan Friedman
Descent • Diane Carey
All Good Things • Michael Jan Friedman
Star Trek: Klingon • Dean W. Smith & Kristine K. Rusch
Star Trek VII: Generations • J. M. Dillard
Metamorphosis • Jean Lorrah
Vendetta • Peter David
Reunion • Michael Jan Friedman
Imzadi • Peter David
The Devil's Heart • Carmen Carter
Dark Mirror • Diane Duane
Q-Squared • Peter David
Crossover • Michael Jan Friedman
Kahless • Michael Jan Friedman
Star Trek: First Contact • J. M. Dillard
The Best and the Brightest • Susan Wright
Planet X • Michael Jan Friedman

#1 *Ghost Ship* • Diane Carey
#2 *The Peacekeepers* • Gene DeWeese
#3 *The Children of Hamlin* • Carmen Carter
#4 *Survivors* • Jean Lorrah
#5 *Strike Zone* • Peter David
#6 *Power Hungry* • Howard Weinstein
#7 *Masks* • John Vornholt
#8 *The Captains' Honor* • David and Daniel Dvorkin
#9 *A Call to Darkness* • Michael Jan Friedman
#10 *A Rock and a Hard Place* • Peter David
#11 *Gulliver's Fugitives* • Keith Sharee
#12 *Doomsday World* • David, Carter, Friedman & Greenberg
#13 *The Eyes of the Beholders* • A. C. Crispin
#14 *Exiles* • Howard Weinstein
#15 *Fortune's Light* • Michael Jan Friedman
#16 *Contamination* • John Vornholt
#17 *Boogeymen* • Mel Gilden

Star Trek: Deep Space Nine®

Star Trek®: Voyager™

Flashback • Diane Carey
The Black Shore • Greg Cox
Mosaic • Jeri Taylor

#1 *Caretaker* • L. A. Graf
#2 *The Escape* • Dean W. Smith & Kristine K. Rusch
#3 *Ragnarok* • Nathan Archer
#4 *Violations* • Susan Wright
#5 *Incident at Arbuk* • John Greggory Betancourt
#6 *The Murdered Sun* • Christie Golden
#7 *Ghost of a Chance* • Mark A. Garland & Charles G.
   McGraw
#8 *Cybersong* • S. N. Lewitt
#9 *Invasion #4: The Final Fury* • Dafydd ab Hugh
#10 *Bless the Beasts* • Karen Haber
#11 *The Garden* • Melissa Scott
#12 *Chrysalis* • David Niall Wilson
#13 *The Black Shore* • Greg Cox
#14 *Marooned* • Christie Golden
#15 *Echoes* • Dean W. Smith & Kristine K. Rusch
#16 *Seven of Nine* • Christie Golden
#17 *Death of a Neutron Star* • Eric Kotani

Star Trek®: New Frontier

#1 *House of Cards* • Peter David
#2 *Into the Void* • Peter David
#3 *The Two-Front War* • Peter David
#4 *End Game* • Peter David
#5 *Martyr* • Peter David
#6 *Fire on High* • Peter David

Star Trek®: Day of Honor

Book One: *Ancient Blood* • Diane Carey
Book Two: *Armageddon Sky* • L. A. Graf
Book Three: *Her Klingon Soul* • Michael Jan Friedman
Book Four: *Treaty's Law* • Dean W. Smith & Kristine K. Rusch

Star Trek®: The Captain's Table

Star Trek®: The Dominion War

Star Trek®: My Brother's Keeper

STARTING THIS JUNE...

An astonishing six-part saga covering
three decades of history from
Star Trek: The Next Generation

One Peaceful Galaxy...

One Deadly Threat...

One Group of Heroes...

Six books. One unforgettable story.

Published by Pocket Books

POCKET
BOOKS

2088